BETRAYED

Tale of a Rogue Surgeon

Satbir Chadha

Vitasta
Let Knowledge Spread

Published by
Renu Kaul Verma
Vitasta Publishing Pvt Ltd
2/15, Ansari Road, Daryaganj
New Delhi-110 002
info@vitastapublishing.com

ISBN 978-93-86473-15-8

Disclaimer
All persons portrayed in this book are fictitious. Any resemblance to real persons, living or dead, is purely co-incidental. Though this is a work of fiction, opinions expressed in it are the author's own. The publisher is in no way responsible for these.

Cover and layout by Vits Press
Printed by Vikas Computer and Printers

Dedication

This book is dedicated to all those who have devoted themselves to medical research over centuries, which have made our lives so comfortable with the advances in medicine, surgery, and therapy over years, eradicating some life threatening diseases, providing relief in chronic conditions, helping us to live longer and productively without pain.

This book is dedicated to practitioners of the noblest profession, whom we reach out to when in illness, before we even reach out to God.

Acknowledgement

My sincere thanks to Renu Kaul Verma of Vitasta Publishing who saw a chapter of this book three years ago, was impressed and urged me to complete the novel. My son Sarabjit, who is my mentor and also my greatest critic; my editor Veena Batra who tolerated my erratic time schedules, I respect her a lot. My family to whom I owe all the chaos in my life, also all the fun and adventure—I am grateful to them for all the love, understanding, financial support and independence they bestow on me. My friends, and regular supporters, Dr Koshy A V, Dr Santosh Bakaya, Dr Vinita Narula, Kiren Babal, and my grandson Paramraj, a fledgling writer himself.

Above all, my husband, Balbir Singh, for his love and faith in me, and my Guruji, Guru Granth Sahib ji, for His blessings.

Anita

AMIT AND I had been together for ever and ever. Mom says we shared the same bathtub, pram and the crib, even the milk bottle when Amit's mom and mine went to the movies. What was a shared nipple when two young ladies were engrossed in the melodrama going on on the screen, soaking their handkerchiefs with tears, while the hero and heroine sang songs of love, longing and desire. We were classmates, teammates, 'hide behind the hedge' mates, and went on to study science in college. Then I split. Not with Amit, but with science; I was not meant for it. I realized I had to become an artist. I had no choice. My heart, my head, my shoulders and my hands would ache and throb, until I put whatever I had conjured into forms. Shapes and colours blurred my eyes till they were applied to canvas. Amit went on to medical college; I studied and practised art. It had to do with my soul, above my mind and reasoning. Though the doctor's white coat and life-giving injections, symbols of my medical ambition as I grew up, were a part of my being, before I gave them up for a paint brush. Ultimately, the medical syringe came to be represented in every piece of my work, however imperceptibly. It was always there with all its multitude of symbolic meanings, phallic and otherwise, differently perceived by me and the viewer.

After my first year exams, I was assigned to look after an aunt recovering from surgery in the city's premium hospital, medical college and research centre, as I was 'free anyway'. This was ages before there were so many reliable private hospitals, and to get treated by a good doctor, you had to be related to his cook or driver or hair-cutter, or you had to have 'pull'. Well, aunt Geeta just had pull, so there she was, getting post-operative care and feeling awfully privileged. I sat around most of the day, walking around the hallowed corridors of the institution when aunty slept, leaving for home at night when a special maid came in to take over the night duty from the day maid. Getting a trained day nurse and night nurse was easy, but costly. The class IV staff in the hospital had to be cajoled into arranging these maids at a fourth of the cost. They took care of the patients well, and the hospital nurses were there anyway for the medicines, injections and other trained care. Maya was the night maid, and on day three, I had begun to get restless after a hugely dull day, so I prepared to leave as she came in. But I delayed my departure by a few minutes so as not to seem uncaring to aunty while I made sure she had everything she needed. Maya had all the useless instructions I could give her. A middle-aged and fat man in khakee uniform passed by. He looked sternly at Maya and said, "Haazree laga de aakey", meaning, come and sign your attendance register. I sat down and told Maya to go, and I would wait.

" I'll do it tomorrow for both days," she said, and he replied, "how about getting one day's salary after working two days?" and left. Reluctantly, she followed him, and returned more than an hour later, to my reprimand. The next evening when she came in, I asked her to sign the register before starting to work, but she evaded me, dextrously filling the water in the flask, and fluffing up the bed. Again the man came by with the same rejoinder, and again she was gone for a long time. I hurried home after she came, but when I bent over my canvas that night, all I could see were her eyes. I became aware of them only then...they were all I could see that night, deep and purposeful, stoic and courageous, but hot as flames. She seemed to be in tearing pain, as if her whole being had been ravaged. But pain is bigger than any anger, and it showed as I struggled through my canvas, debating with the colours. I slept after having painted only a huge pair of eyes; soulful, painful eyes, coloured in the dark waters of the river, and the orange of the setting sun, with deep shadows beneath.

Next evening, the man in khakee was there before I could begin a meaningful conversation with Maya, as I had planned. To a young under-graduate, after identifying someone in pain, the next step is to try and alleviate it, and my enthusiastic youth believed that every pain could be eradicated somehow. Maya asked him to go ahead, she would follow. I said to her, "Why don't you go on and be done with it? Go on and sign your register, and I need to talk to you when you get back."

"Why should I have to go every day? It's not as if I am making thousands of rupees. I am poor, but how much should I suffer?" Maya almost cried.

"Come on Maya, it is only your attendance, it is good to have a regular record," I patted her as she pulled away and hissed at me, "Didi, how can you not understand? There is no register. That man wants to have sex with us in return for appointing us for one day's duty in the ward. We are not permanent employees, and get employed as temporary staff for a few days in a month, at this man's whims and fancies. If I don't please him, he will call in another maid, and maybe not give me work for a long time. All maids know about it but no one can complain for we need the work." And then came the old philosophy, "If we have to enjoy respect and dignity, we have to be born rich; poor fools have no business to dream about it even. We should be grateful if we can eat and have a roof over our heads."

I was so stunned by her speech, I forgot to swallow. My jaw drooped as Mom came in to look at aunty. Quietly I made my way out of the room to absorb slowly what I had heard, to believe it, and later to come to terms with it. How could this be happening here, in the Mecca of the noblest profession, this place that proudly sends out the best doctors? How could it be happening at all? I found the senior nurse and took her into confidence. I told her I wanted to make a complaint, but she said, "Why? Does Maya think she is a princess? We all make compromises. And you please don't mess up things for us. If you make a complaint, Maya will stop getting work, then how will she pay her childrens' school fees?"

"Getting work at what cost? She will find a way to make honest money; we ought to help her," I continued.

"Listen, let's talk tomorrow, I have work to complete." 'Tomorrow', mysteriously, I was no longer required to be with Aunty, and over some days the outrage of the day got relegated to the weaker areas of my memory, and life moved on.

I shared the experience with Amit when he came for the weekend, and he said, "Now you're so upset, but when I shared with you how I was ragged in Medical College—you laughed; it was so much fun for you. I was assaulted continuously for a month. Almost all the seniors took turns, even the girls did not spare me. Stop yourself now. When one can do nothing about the system, it's better not to talk about the issue. We can discuss the problem endlessly, but unproductive discussion is as futile as foreplay without making love." And we talked of other things—his studies, future dreams, my work, the weather, and cinema.

I graduated from Art College, and got an interesting project to work on, planning the art display in the lobby of an upcoming five star hotel. When I began, I thought of it as a very pleasant place, with an atmosphere of comfort and beauty. Then I did a study of the prospective visitors to the place, and the projected clientele. The statistics were not much different from the statistics about the type of people visiting any other place, be it the market, the railway station, the airport, or hospital. Happiness and suffering, joys and sorrows, satisfaction and unrest, success and failure, are equally distributed to the human race, over all classes and ages. I decided to remember this when designing the lobby—a beautiful place has to have a perfect projection of all human emotions, and the shapes and colours that go with them. I filled my syringe with the colours of life, and injected life in my work. Meanwhile, Amit began his internship, in the same hospital where I had spent time with Aunty. I would spend a day there sometimes, to be with Amit, and to observe people. The hospital was full of suffering but it was also full of hope, denial, and also acceptance.

The gynaecology ward was the most interesting, with all the women chatting all the time. They simply had to describe their lives for everyone, their pain and their struggles. Their joys and their hopes had to be shared, and the experiences of others had to be known about. I think it made the pain less, and the future brighter, just talking so much about it. Also, as I realize now, there were no television sets in hospital wards then, and no mobile phones either, making conversation the only entertainment. Then, there was this corner ward, with twenty women, which had no number or status written on the door, and very few doctors or nurses going in and out of it—just one nurse sitting on duty inside the ward, and, strangely, the women hardly talking to each other. Some very young ones, teenagers actually, had a mother or sister accompanying them—but most women were essentially alone. Surprisingly, this was a very quiet ward. Occasionally, a woman could be heard sobbing, or groaning. Most were clutching their stomach, or tossing in bed holding tight the metal rods at the head of the bed.

Being Amit's fiancée, (though we were not formally engaged, it was simply taken for granted that we were engaged), I had a run of the place. After several small conversations with the patients in the ward, and the nurses, but chiefly the women who came in the most often to clean the two washrooms shared by all the women, I gathered a lot of information. Sharda would stub her 'beedi' just outside the ward before going in, and light a new one as she stepped out after cleaning the washroom, so I targeted her. I offered her a tip of ten rupees for 'beedi', and started talking. "You should give up smoking, you know, it is bad for the lungs. One gets TB and even cancer from smoking so much."

"Ha! The doctors have a cigarette hanging from their mouths all the time, and nothing happens to them, so how can a small beedi harm me?"

"Tell me Sharda, how long have you been working here?"

"Since I got married. It was my mother-in-law's job, and she passed it on to me." I kept on, "Oh, you must have been her favourite." "Obviously, no one worked as hard as me. I did everything possible to please her, I even gave her my gold chain that my husband got me; after all, if Ma was wearing silver, how could I wear gold? She really loved me."

" I see you have a heart of gold. Tell me what are these women being treated for in this ward? I think, after so many years you know so much, you are almost a doctor yourself."

"Of course," she said, "the doctors do so much book learning, but we learn the practical way, by observing the doctors and nurses, and when we offer to do some tasks for them, they actually teach us some tricks also. You will be surprised—I can give simple injections, take the temperature and blood-pressure, and even do normal deliveries. Experience makes you perfect. In my locality, I am often called to do deliveries; they believe I am a midwife. You know poor women cannot afford a hospital, specially when they are having a baby almost every year, so I go to their house and deliver. I make good money too." I was shocked, and wondered how anyone could be so reckless.

"Now tell me about this ward. I just cannot understand what these women are being treated for."

"Naturally you can't." Sharda was on a roll now. "It is a secret research. A woman with an unwanted pregnancy will go to any limit to end it. Here, after a general check-up, the lady doctor gives the pregnant woman two pills to swallow on an empty stomach in the morning, and assigns her a bed to lie on. After some hours, the woman begins to get labour pains, slowly increasing in intensity till they become unbearable. Ultimately, it is like a natural abortion. When the pushing of the muscles is strong, she is guided to go to the bathroom, and the foetus is pushed out as she squats on the lavatory. Then she informs the nurse, who checks to see if the foetus is really out, and calls one of us to clean the washroom. The patient gradually gets relief from the pain, and after some time she is given food, and some pain-killers. Six hours after she has aborted, she is sent away after giving her some vitamins to take for some days."

These were obviously the 'morning-after pills' that are sold over-the-counter these days. Trials on humans were being conducted, but on unsuspecting poor women, it seemed.

"What if something goes wrong, if the abortion is incomplete, or the pills don't work for someone or if there is a reaction or something—how are the patients cared for then?"

"Things do go wrong sometimes; in that case, the women are advised to get admitted to the hospital formally, and they are treated by the gynaecologists."

I persisted, "Don't their families quarrel with the doctors? Aren't these people afraid of having legal action taken against them?"

"Who will fight for these women? Most of them are prostitutes, sex-workers, some are unwed young girls who are brought here to hush up their condition; even older married women who have a relationship out of marriage. People will abandon these women rather than fight for them, they are of easy virtue anyway. Some cases are really sad. Young girls who have seen nothing in life, like that Preeti on bed number eight—she has been brought here for the second time in six months."

Shocked, I went towards the bed and found a young girl, almost a child, groaning with pain, and her mother rubbing her back, while her own tears flowed unchecked.

I asked her, "How old is Preeti?"

She burst into fresh tears as she said, "only thirteen."

"Then you should check on her boy friend and teach her good values; this procedure is so risky, she could lose her life."

"No boy friend, Didi, she is home all the time. She never even goes to play. Her own uncle does this to her, she has yet to learn about life. Poor girl, she does not know what has happened to her, and why she is here, and what is being done. She thinks she has a very hard stool to pass, and there is something wrong with her digestion."

"Then why don't you protect her? Can't your husband take his brother to task, and see that he cannot harm her?"

"My husband? I dare not let him know anything."

"But you must for Preeti's sake."

"He will only blame my child and maybe even kill her. We live in the same house with my brother-in-law, and I go to work as a domestic help. I lock Preeti in the room when I go out, but somehow that wretched man gets to catch her."

I pondered and said, "Will you be willing to let Preeti come home with me. I can assure you she will be very safe, and I shall arrange school education also for her. She can help my mother with some housework, and we will pay you well. You can also come to meet her when you want."

She wept some more and thanked me, while I promised to take Preeti away next morning from the hospital itself. I felt satisfied that I could help one young girl at least. When I went next morning, there was no sign of Preeti or her mother. I asked the nurse on duty where they were, and she said she didn't know. I threatened to create a scene, and insisted to know, and she said, "I really do not know where they live. No one knows. Initially we kept registers, tried to contact the women, even for research purposes, but we realized that they almost always gave us false names and addresses. You can see what category of women come for this treatment—they are either the nameless scum of society, or women hiding their sin from their families. They always come alone, having heard of this place from friends or someone. We did target the red light areas for our research and spread the word that we were helping with unwanted pregnancies; we explained the nature of our work to women who came in, but they were least interested. They just want an easy, non-surgical method of abortion, which is also free. I am sorry, I can't help you more than that. Even if I was allowed to give you Preeti's address, I am sure you will find that neither is Preeti her real name, nor is her address correct. Even today, we have in the ward six 'Preetis' and eight 'Sonias', so you can guess how many are real."

This left me so disturbed, I could not sleep for many nights. I hated Amit's profession; I hated the poverty in my country; I hated myself for being so blessed and fortunate. And my canvas was full of the colours of fire, and blood, and the deep colour of pain; and the syringe spewed forth foetuses of many shapes and sizes, but all throbbing, and all red, on to the blotched white background of hospital sheets.

A happy sojourn and a wedding

I NEVER got to do the design for the lobby of the five star hotel. I was told I had no sense of aesthetics. I wanted to do the project quite desperately, to prove to myself that I was a professional artist, but my idea of beauty conflicted with that of the management. They wanted to tell me what goes in the design, and I said that I believed that it was to be my design. I realized the futility of an argument, and resigned before even having joined.

Meanwhile, Amit began his post graduation and senior residency, and had no time for me or for himself. Sulking took away a good part of my day, and soon I was stagnating; so I decided to travel and see new places and people, particularly hill people. I had never lived in the hills, and always found them exhilarating. Naini Tal was the place I chose to be my base for I had a friend who belonged there and had a family and a house there too. The first time I saw Naini Tal, I thought it could not be real, it just had to be a huge painting; the beauty of the place took my breath away. The hills were green, a deep thick green, with a house here and a house there, with colourful flowers around and sloping red roofs; one could actually count the houses, and the locals identified each house by its owner's name. The scent in the air was almost tangible, and the lake was so green too, with ducks swimming across in a single file to the sunny side, and beautiful, colourful boats, idling in a neat row.

I occupied a room in my friend's house, for the family's hospitality would never let them accept rent from anyone, and as I lived there I learnt that it was the custom there. People living there would welcome any number of relatives and friends into their houses, especially in the summers when the plains were sweltering with heat, actually feeling offended if the guests even mentioned a hotel. They would happily feed them and load them with gifts when they were ready to leave, making them promise that they would come again soon. 'Wow', I thought, 'such generosity you cannot even think of in the city.'

I walked around Naini Tal everyday. It was such a sparkling clean town, I thought I could go without a change of clothes for a month. But I hardly painted. The boats on the lake, the hills and the clouds, already looked like a painting, there was no point copying it. So I began to go to other small towns nearby, higher up in the hills, and in the beautiful valleys. Though every valley astounded me with the different colours of nature, and how a passing cloud would change all the colours, and the mountain breeze would make whole hillsides sway, it was the people there whom I transferred to my canvas. The chubby children with rosy cheeks, the old men and women with deeply grooved faces and crinkling eyes, rich skin, glowing with a permanent tan, young boys and girls, all were immensely beautiful. There seemed to be no obesity at all, and the people walked very straight with a particular gait, thrusting their shoulders before their bodies while going uphill, which I could not copy, though I felt it would cause less exhaustion for the weight of the body was spread a bit.

I guess one needed the practice of decades of hill climbing to achieve that gait. Also the way these people would squat on their haunches for hours, defying arthritis. I painted the women toiling in the fields, the men grazing sheep, and groups of older men and women squatting in a circle smoking their 'beedis'. Every few days, I needed to go to Naini Tal to restock my paints and canvases, and draw money from the bank. On this particular trip to Naini Tal, there were other guests visiting my friend's family, and I was requested to escort them to see the scenery from 'Snow View', a popular tourist point. All went well, but on the return journey, while walking back, I slipped and fell. There was a pony trotting down the slope with a toddler on its back, and as I rolled over to avoid coming in its path, I went flying down the hill to the road, some seven feet below, and fractured my leg. The bone snapped like a twig and the jarred end could be seen through the skin. I refused to get up and asked to be taken to a hospital immediately, but the guests knew nothing of the place, and would have had to walk back and get someone from my friend's house which would take an hour at least, while I was crying in pain. Luckily, an officer passed by in his jeep, and took me to the hospital. The doctor in charge saw the condition I was in, and admitted me at once to the ward. He said the senior doctor would come in some time. My companions went back to make a call to my parents, for I would certainly need my family by my side now.

Now began my most horrible, and painful experience in a hospital. Starting from the afternoon, I lay groaning and weeping in bed, it was sheer agony. My friend's relatives came back in the evening, getting me food that I could not eat anyway. But there was no sign of any senior doctor. Every time I requested, or screamed for a doctor, the junior resident came in and apologised, saying it would take some more time. Night fell, and there was still no senior doctor. Someone instructed the junior doctor to give me a Pethidine injection, to help with the pain. I am sure it must have been given so that I would get some sleep and not disturb the other patients in the ward. I could not control my frustration, my anger, disappointment too, for what do you do in a hospital without a doctor to help you, when your problem is so obviously intense and urgent. I had never felt so helpless in my life.

Next morning, at 4.30 am, Dad arrived, having travelled by the night bus. Seeing him, I started to cry like a child. Even he could not believe that I was lying there unattended since the previous afternoon. He went chasing the staff that was available, and gave them a piece of his mind, but realized that nothing could be done till the senior doctor in charge of the hospital came in. But his investigations with the lower staff revealed a terrible truth: the doctor had spent the previous day writing reports of the 'Vasectomies' he had performed during last week, the incentive money he had disbursed, and other details.

We were stunned. How could he have been making reports when people like me were suffering? Infection could have set in and the delay in the treatment could have caused permanent damage to the fractured tissues; only doctors are supposed to know what complications could have arisen.

And the civil surgeon of the district was busy writing reports of 'Vasectomies'?

By then, the junior doctor came again to tell me that I should go 'nil by mouth' (fasting), for my leg had to be plastered. I said, "How could this decision have been taken when the doctor has not even seen me?"

And he said, "Madam, I have been informing him. Please do not be upset, now-a-days it is so. It is mandatory to perform the stipulated number of Vasectomies every week, and if the report does not go on time, Sir can be suspended or transferred to some obscure place. We are living in an 'Emergency' you know. Even if we do not cure a single patient, our hundred Vasectomies have to be done, and duly reported."

I was shocked and I told him, "Why did you not tell me yesterday? I would have gone to the *Zanana* (ladies) hospital. At least I would have got some help."

"No madam, you would get no help, for the doctor there also has to do the required number of 'Tubectomies' or the sterilising of women, and make the reports. She has even less time than Sir. We are living in an Emergency you know. But don't worry, Sir will come at ten o'clock and plaster your leg and then you will be fine. I am sorry for the delay."

"Listen," I said, "the Emergency means that our country is under threat from people trying to disrupt the government, or damage our administration; how does it mean that doctors have to only sterilise people and not treat the sick ones?"

"I am a government servant, Madam, I cannot comment. The people in Delhi are committed to reducing the growth rate of our country's population, and we doctors have been given orders to sterilise a certain number of people every week, if we are to remain in service."

"But how many women and men are there in these scantily populated hills of the productive age that you can sterilise?"

"We do not bother whether they are productive or not; we send out agents to collect men and get them here, and there is a financial incentive offered, too. They may get us eighty-year-old widowers, we don't bother, we have to get the numbers, that is all."

I thought of all the handsome men I had met in the tiny villages and towns in the hills, and wondered how many had succumbed to the meagre financial lure and lost their ability to procreate, their liberty to procreate. And how many, like me, had been denied timely treatment in their illness, so that the doctors could fill the files. I had seen the ordeal of getting a sick person to hospital from a village; he would be carried on someone's shoulders till the bus stand, to wait in agony till the bus arrived, then gone through the arduous bus journey, with head banging bumps and losing his balance on the steep curves, then to be carried a further two kilometres up the hill to the hospital, or, if one could afford it, hire a 'Dandee' in which four men carried one passenger on their shoulders, only to toss painfully in bed, because the doctors were busy with their Vasectomies and reports.

I was ultimately wheeled into the X-ray room, and with a wet X-ray to guide the surgeon, into the OT where I passed out under the chloroform. As I was coming out of the ether, I dreamed of spraying the ministers in Delhi and the doctors in Naini Tal with bullets from my syringe.

Some three days later, when my pain was bearable, Dad hired a taxi to take me back home, where I would get better care and rest. Then Amit took over my treatment. He cried buckets having missed me, then the best Orthopaedic did my plaster over again, using better and lighter material. Then Amit announced that as soon as I was well, we both were getting married. This delighted me for I had been really missing Amit. I was ready to move in with him, plaster and all, but we were very orthodox back then. I had tons of questions about the Emergency but was told not to ask; even our freedom of speech had been compromised.

Being immobile turned out to be a good thing. I dreamed a lot. About the new phase of my life with Amit, how much I was going to love him, and also the logistics of the wedding ceremony. Both our parents were planning huge parties, and large gifts of jewellery and dresses, but the Emergency was playing spoilsport for them, there being a restriction on the number of guests one could invite to a wedding. It was dictatorial. Anyway, Amit decided upon a simple wedding, and requested our folks to spend their money on helping us to set up our house, for we had decided to live alone, and not with the family as was the custom. Three months went by in a dream. I was convalescing, so sarees were being brought home for me to chose, ditto with jewellery,·and after the wedding ceremony we got the most pleasant surprise. We were taken to our new home, a two bedroom house, with small verandas in front and behind, bought for us by our kind parents, furnished beautifully, with a well equipped kitchen, a study, and a studio upstairs for me. We were delighted, and emotionally overcome. Then came the bigger surprise. Our friends had pooled in to buy a brand new shining motorcycle for Amit; this filled us with warmth and gratitude. God was so kind.

We didn't need to go on a honeymoon, for we were to be living alone anyway. We moved into our new house just after the wedding. Heaven had to be the size of our apartment. No bliss could have exceeded what we felt there. Amit and me and no one else. Time flew. Burnt meals, semi-cooked 'dal', boiled potatoes with salt, fruits and cookies sent in by our parents, eggs never fried right, these were the treats one ate in heaven. Music and dance. All over the floor, all over the bed, on the open veranda at midnight, sex happened all the time. The hero working shifts at the hospital, the heroine sulking at home; heroine going off to meet parents, hero boiling in frustration; and then making up on the dining table with more sex, what else? These were the rituals of heaven.

When Amit handed me his first stipend, I felt as rich as a queen, and spent the whole day wondering how I was going to spend it; though by evening I realized I wouldn't have much to spend, after the electricity and phone bills, the maid and petrol, and other small stuff. I told that to Amit, and he said, "Ok, pay the maid and the other bills, and we'll simply have sex for breakfast, sex for lunch, and, guess what—sex for dinner. As for food, we can have it over the weekend at our parents."

I told him, "This is what everyone in India does when there isn't enough food, and if there is no money for food, there is no money for contraceptives, so the population multiplies, and there is again less food. I'm sure that is why we are having Emergency in the country. So let's eat over the week and have sex on weekends." And my paintings began to depict physical intimacy, in the blending of the colours, the blending of the forms; the piston in the syringe moving smoothly to pour out pictures full of love—deep love, passionate love, craving for love, dying for love, from orange to purple, pink and red, all hues of love.

This was the beginning of a new life with Amit.

Proudly, a small name plate, designed and painted by me, was fixed on the gate of our house saying 'Dr Amit Biswas MBBS.'

'Mrs Anita Biswas Artist and Designer.'

After this we became famous. People who had looked through us before came visiting us, saying, "Oh! Your husband is a doctor. So noble. Even my son is working hard to be a doctor; maybe he can come sometimes to get guidance and help from your husband." Another one said, "You are just like my own daughter; count on me whenever you need any help; I am so proud my daughter's husband is such a nice doctor." Then people began to come over to consult Amit, and he did not refuse for that was his profession. People refused to understand that our house was not a consulting room; they believed a doctor could be consulted anywhere, anytime. So we added a sliding panel on the nameplate which said "IN" when Amit was free, and "OUT" when he was not. This helped a lot. We had to get a trolley on which Amit could examine his patients, and soon they began to insist that Amit accept some payment, for they said, "We will not feel comfortable otherwise; after all, how many times can we have a free consultation?"

Now Amit was earning more, but had very little free time. When I grumbled, he said, "These folks are enriching my experience, and besides, isn't it a doctor's duty to help the sick and suffering? Remember that doctor in Naini Tal? How bad you felt then." That was that then. I mean only a fool would marry a doctor, a cricketer or a filmstar, and expect privacy in her life. For that one had to marry a shopkeeper.

Then a month later something weird happened, which made us feel as if we were members of some underworld gang, or extortion outfit. A man came cycling up to our gate and asked for Dr Amit Biswas. He handed Amit an envelope, and turned to leave at once. Amit shouted to him to stop, but he said he was in a hurry, and it was his job to only deliver and leave.

"At least tell us who has sent you," Amit said, and he replied, "You will come to know. I cannot stop and I cannot talk to you." And he cycled away. Crisp hundred rupee notes slipped out of the envelope, to our shock, as we wondered if there had been a mistake, or whether we were being set up in some income-tax scoop.

"I don't even earn enough to have to pay income-tax," Amit said, and pondered over the mystery. We worried what damage could happen to Amit's career, for it had to be shady money, considering the way it was remitted. Would Amit be asked to do something unethical, in return for this money? No, he would never do that, come what may; there was some law and order in the country, in spite of the Emergency. He would see his friend's uncle who was high up in the police department. But first, we had to discover where this money had come from. The envelope was put on the mock mantelpiece over a mock fireplace. Houses at the time still made these decorative features in memory of real fireplaces, and we waited for someone to unravel the mystery.

That happened soon enough. While walking in the park next morning, a well groomed man came up and said, "Namaskar, Doctor Sahab, I am Dr Sarthi from Perfect Pathology Lab. I hope my man reached you yesterday. For a beginner, you are doing very well. We will pay you our respects regularly, and count on your co-operation." Amit's face was a picture of surprise and shock, but even as he began to protest, the man hurried away, whispering, "See you another time, we have to be cautious you know." Amit decided to visit his Lab and thrash out things, now that we knew where the envelope had come from. That he did, and continued to go to the Lab for several days, only to be told, "Dr Sarthi is not in." We just could not understand.

"Then who is in charge when he is not there? I wish to meet whoever is the manager here," said Amit.

"Right now no one can see you, we will contact you later," he was told, and that was that. Anyway, one morning again, Mr Sarthi met Amit in the park. "Please do not come to the lab again, you can tell me your problem now, but hurry, I don't wish to be seen with you; its the Emergency and the place is full of policemen in plain clothes."

"But I have done nothing illegal," Amit said. "Our transaction according to the rules is illegal. Any cuts in the medical profession are illegal."

"What cuts? Every time a patient comes for investigations to our lab, we automatically pay twenty per cent to the prescribing doctor. All labs and X-Ray clinics, all have the same rate."

"But I never referred anyone to you or anyone else."

"That is not necessary. Your signature on the prescription is enough."

"But I do not want to receive the cuts. That is the reason I have been visiting your lab. I want to return the money. I am still studying for my specialisation; I just help some neighbours who come in. Please take back the money you have sent, I will not use it; and don't send me anything again."

"That is not possible; our accounting system has been set like that—all doctors get their due, none more and none less. And I shall not be meeting you ever again, and please never mention my name to anyone. If you happen to see me, ignore me. Goodbye."

And he was gone. Amit and I were more perturbed now. Amit carefully brought up the topic with a senior, and was told that it was the universally accepted kickback; it was part of the system, and why was Amit trying to fight it. Months went by, with more patients, more investigations, and more envelopes coming in. How long would they last on the mantelpiece? Soon the currency poured into our wallets. It spelt the difference between straining the means and having ample funds, between being neatly dressed and being elegantly dressed, between perpetual vegetarianism and frequent fish meals, between an occasional coke and an occasional beer; major changes for a small salary earner. The voice of conscience is a very soft voice, when we begin to ignore it, gradually whimpering away to silence. It is loud when we are content, and we can afford to listen to it without fastening any belts. It is a really loyal pet. My easels and paints were so costly too.

Meanwhile, the Emergency simply dragged on, bringing fresh assaults everyday on different parts of society. There were pictures in the newspapers of a particular civil servant, who began to be known as the 'bulldozer man', wearing thick specs, bulldozing a cluster of hutments one day, and bulldozing an established market on another; ordering people to break down the front of their shops and make them all identical, with identically painted boards, and people quietly doing it. Was he trying to plant date palms in Siberia? How can you make Indian cities look like London? Everything was stupefying—the worst was the lack of the liberties that we had been used to. We were cautious about what we spoke and to whom—anyone could be an informer, or one could just be misrepresented. This was not our India, this was a paranoid country, very alien to our culture, where we were used to calling in unknown people for a cup of tea, saying, "How can you go without some hospitality?" Something terrible was going on. And just when we began to think that it would never end, there was a huge uprising, and the government saw better sense and the Emergency ended. Our spirits soared, and how. We began to breathe the air of freedom, to laugh aloud, to cheer after so long. We were not richer, but we definitely lived in a brighter country now.

The media went berserk with rejuvenated freedom; my paintings too acquired a whole new colour scheme. I began to experiment with absurd shapes and forms, stark colours, and enjoyed the brightness of white like never before. And the paintings started to sell well, too. I would share exhibitions with other new painters, and often sold a couple of pieces at a good price. I learnt that the higher the price you ask for a painting, the higher the interest it generates in the viewers, and the quicker it sells, but it should be good too, and ultimately it is the viewer's perception and aesthetic intelligence that decides what he will buy. But I was encouraged, and happy. I made many friends among the artists' fraternity. Most evenings were now spent meeting them over coffee, frequent browsing at various venues, inspiring conversation. I was loving my life.

Meanwhile, Amit was completing his post graduation, specialising as an orthopaedic surgeon, not such a popular stream then, for any surgeon could set a fracture, so it was believed. He was assisting his senior, Dr Subrot, who had been his mentor for two years. Dr Subrot trusted Amit enough to allow him to do complete surgeries in Dr Subrot's name, thus gaining immense experience and expertise. Socially too, Dr Subrot liked having Amit with him on almost all occasions—family functions, medical seminars, or weekend gatherings. After Amit cleared the exams and was officially given the degree of MD Orthopaedics, Dr Subrot invited us to a very special weekend party, for now we were one of them and Amit would be practising independently. I had just conceived, and did not feel fit enough to go. Even my mother had advised me not to venture out much from home, "Caution," she said, "is better than regret later." And with such a precious cargo, even I was not taking any chances. Amit was eager to please his Subrot Sir, but I declined, and he had to go all alone. He returned next morning, and was in such a daze, I was shocked. I nagged him to tell me what had happened, but he was reluctant, though by afternoon he could not hold it any longer, and blurted out, "You won't believe me Anita, what happened at the party. I went with Subrot Sir to a huge bungalow far from the city, with lush green lawns, landscaped gardens, stunning patches of flowers, and a private swimming pool. The top doctors of the city were there—surgeons, cardiologists, gynaecologists, neurologists—I was overawed. Some of them I knew. Sir introduced me to the others, and kept telling everyone that I have a very charming and talented wife who is an artist. I blushed. Everyone was disappointed that you were not with me. I told them you were in the family way, and they congratulated me. Music played softly and drinks kept coming on with loads of rich snacks, the kind I have never tasted before. There was lots of joking and laughter and the drinks were loosening up the talk, and even vulgar jokes were being shared. All the doctors were laughing. The same people who are so rigid and upright otherwise, were having fun like teenagers at a college social, but I thought everyone needs to let their hair down sometimes.

"Slowly the music got louder and faster, everyone was dancing like mad, partners were changing, steps were erratic, there was more fumbling and fondling than dancing. Then around midnight, two waiters came in carrying trays with some capsules and some pills, and served them around.

Some guests took pills, some took capsules, and some took a combination of both. I pretended to swallow a pill; I dared not take anything for I did not know what it may be. Then a huge screen lit up, and a pornographic movie was projected with a powerful projector. By then I think all the guests were very high. I don't think any of them were in their senses. It was really weird; I was both stunned and shocked, and could not believe it was happening, or that I was a part of it. Whenever Sir passed me by, he would say, 'Cheer up man, loosen up and enjoy.' Slowly they all began to take off their clothes—all of them—men and women. Like the actors in the film, most men had erections and it was a complete orgy. One could not see who was making out with whom, and nobody bothered either. Some couples were having sex on sofas, some on the floor, some walked into the swimming pool, completely nude, and many of them were doing threesomes and some foursomes. Seeing them in the throes of so much unnatural passion, devilish energy pervading them all, I became disgusted. Nobody was aware of my presence anymore, so I sneaked out into the hall, and surprisingly, the hall showed no sign of what was happening inside. I reclined on a sofa and soon fell asleep. I had drunk many times more than I had ever drunk. I woke up when a number of waiters trooped in carrying trays with cups and teapots. I realized the movie had been turned off. When I peeped into the party hall, folks were lying asleep, semi-dressed or nude, as may have been the situation when they passed out ultimately. For a moment, that scene reminded me of our mortuary with bodies of different shapes and sizes lying immobile. A bell went off, and I walked out as they began to awake and pull themselves together, but within an hour they all came to the hall freshened and spruced up, impeccable pictures of dignity. It was amazing. The bonhomie persisted, and compliments were passed about the drinks and snacks, and the party generally. They were all fresh again.

"Sir said the party was very well organised. Breakfast was quickly served in the hall, which all ate greedily, and speedily took their leave. On the way back, I confessed to Sir that I had not been comfortable, but he said, 'Amit, we doctors are under immense pressure twenty-four hours a day, every day. When you reach my level of practice you will understand. Even while sleeping, we are alert—emergencies happen round the clock. Once in a while, we too need to unwind, to get some recreation. The tougher the pressures in our lives, the tougher the measures to relieve them. We have to totally lose ourselves, to become fresh again. If the release is not there, our mental faculties will slow down, reducing our performance professionally. And permanently living under pressure will make us sick. Senior professionals everywhere keep finding smarter ways to unwind. It's normal, son. Relax.' This is an account, Anita, of last night's party, and I regret that I ever went. I am feeling disgraced already."

"You are not guilty. Relax and come for lunch." But I was far from relaxed; actually I was terribly apprehensive. Very, very apprehensive. It was a crucial period of my life. I was expecting my first baby, blooming as an artist, and my husband was at the threshold of a promising career. But something changed. Amit changed. Gone was the simple, ambitious young man, gone were the noble aspirations; he looked like a cub who had had the first taste of blood, and who knew nothing would be enough again. I could feel the shift from a good healing doctor to a famous, prosperous, successful and renowned surgeon that the new Amit looked to be in the future. I was not comfortable with this new person, but I was tied to him for life, and I loved him. Loved him more than I could ever love myself, had always loved him, and would always love him.

The pregnancy that had delighted me, now gave me nightmares; the syringe squirted embryos, red and palpitating, and I imagined Amit with various women, fondling them; it was terrible. Amit noticed it and I shared my demons with him; I guess I had forgotten that Amit loved me as much as I loved him. He took great care of me now, rubbing the back of my neck to relax me, and scratching my back to help me sleep. He generally spent all spare time with me so I never felt neglected. And the human mind is so vulnerable, a little sweetness takes so much bitterness away, while small doubts can create so much hatred. With Amit's arms around me, I was really reassured. Amit said this baby was very lucky for him for he was getting surgery cases almost everyday, and making lots of money. I reminded him of his resolve to treat poor patients free, but he said, "That will come later, darling; I need to save loads of money to begin my own practice, my own clinic; after all, how long can I remain Subrot Sir's assistant?" I knew then that my Amit had grown too big, and the old one was never coming back. Money and success drove him now. He wanted to be like the very successful doctors he had met at the party; he wanted to be a part of their circle. I understood that, and despite all the conflicts in my mind, accepted him this way too. After all, as he said, "I would be enjoying the goodies too."

Mohini

MOHINI WAS all of fourteen years old, of dark complexion, tall but with a straight back. Her head seemed small for her lanky body, which swayed from the hips when she walked, and she walked with long swift strides, as though each step had a purpose. She could not be said to have a pretty face, for her nose was too broad, and lips too thick—they formed a circle together. But her sharp eyes held all of one's attention; intelligent, confident, and utterly emotional. And her eyes gave that sexy soft look that almost held your hand in friendship. She had studied up to class seven, and then had been stopped from further education. This was Punjab in 1946, the part that is now in Pakistan; and the village folk were enjoying a benign winter, with fields loaded with grain, the landscape only green and gold, and the clear blue of the cloudless sky. The Second World War had been over more than a year ago, and the country was full of anticipation—anticipation of freedom from the British rule of over two centuries.

Punjab gave the British army thousands of fine soldiers who had fought battles all over the world, and the survivors were back to well deserved rest and pampering by their families. Those who did not return were remembered proudly as heroes, and their families enjoyed ample pensions too. Mohini's parents were farmers, like almost everyone in Punjab, and though not the richest, were very comfortable. Mohini was the pampered elder daughter, with two younger brothers. Class seven was considered 'highly educated' back then, and her parents feared that she would not get a fitting husband if she studied further, for boys were less likely to stick to school for long, farming taking them away to the fields quite young.

Mohini did feel the stirrings and yearning of a teenager, and had very early known about the birds and the bees, growing up with the cattle in the family, and what with sleeping on rooftops during the long summer months that lasted more than half the year. She felt nice when proposals were discussed for her hand. She had felt attracted to some of the young boys in the village; had seen her friends disappearing behind the swaying corn with their lovers, but she had too much integrity and character to risk losing her virginity; she had decided that she would wait for the man chosen by her parents, marry him, and create her happiness. Soon her match was fixed. She was to marry Satnam, a young lad from the same village, the youngest of three brothers, the elder two were already married. Satnam was a Matriculate, and had let it be known that he aspired to join the army, like many in Punjab, having listened with rapt attention to the stories narrated by the old soldiers, of wars in distant lands like Burma, Japan and even Germany.

The village elders listened to BBC radio for news, for there was tension around about the pending independence, and rumours that the country was to be divided unbelievably into two separate countries for Muslims and Hindus.

The simple people could not understand the politics, but a refrain of fear could be heard about the unpredictability of the near future. In the likelihood of having to shift to the Hindu part of India, most families were marrying off their children especially those who were betrothed, for in that culture marrying off your children was the biggest responsibility, and once that was done, one's life was considered fulfilled.

Those were very confused times politically, especially for the rustic apolitical folks. So Mohini's wedding was held within two months of the betrothal, and before the wheat cropping season, when there are massive celebrations on the festival of 'Baisakhi'.

Carrying a flurry of emotions in her bosom, sad at parting from her family, but eager to be with Satnam, whom she had begun to love as her husband already, though she had never seen him, Mohini, the young bride, entered her new home full of hope, excitement and love for everyone in the new family. All day she sat in the family courtyard with other women of the family, while almost the whole village came to bless her. Her mother-in-law was the first to lift her veil to see her daughter-in-law's face for the first time. She duly blessed her. And after allowing her other two daughters-in-law to get a peep-eye, she ordered that the new bride was not to be disturbed to show her face to anyone else for the day. Most visitors wrinkled their noses and said, "Obviously the bride is not beautiful," while some also said, "it is wise for you never know who may cast an evil eye on their happiness. And we'll all get to meet her by and by."

After sunset no one came, and the close family had a tremendous feast; there was mutton curry and roasted quails which some relatives had gone hunting for the day before; great Basmati Pulao with cold 'Phirni'. And the liquor was served in pails; one could ask for a jug-full or a tumbler-full—these were the peg-sizes. The women sat together singing naughty songs, mainly about the manipulative mother-in-law being the major obstacle between the newly-wed husband and wife. All very hilarious. The men danced a vigorous 'Bhangra' till they could stand no more. A joyful celebration for the family till some wise old ladies directed the elder two daughters-in-law to take the new couple to their room so they could retire. Even this was done ceremoniously. Satnam was taken first and left there; then Mohini was taken by them, carrying a two litre jug of milk for her husband—a cute custom—an offering of the purest food God has created, supposed to keep you fortified for the most ardent night of your life.

Mohini bent to touch her husband's feet, and he lifted her up and took her in his arms. "I wish you to lie on my bosom, not at my feet, my dear. I am an educated man, and respect women. Come, let me look at my wife's beautiful face," he said as he lifted her veil.

She was astonished to see how handsome he was. He was tall with broad shoulders and a lean body. His complexion was brown, tanned by the winter sun; she could see it glow in the light of the kerosene lantern. He had sharp features, his nose was aquiline like a Pathan's with brown eyes, brown beard and moustaches. He seemed to be both tough and soft at the same time.

"I am sorry, I am no beauty, you will be disappointed," Mohini mumbled, but he began to kiss her on the lips.

Mohini said, "I have such ugly lips, and nose, and you are so handsome, I feel guilty."

But Satnam continued to kiss her, more and more passionately, saying, "Your lips are like 'gulab-jamun' to me, so sweet and syrupy. I love you Mohini, and will love you always." As he sat her on the bed, she suddenly wanted to wrap herself around him, and have him all around her. Her passion rose, and she quickly wanted him between her legs. All night they made ardent, immature love, exploring, caressing, till a light rap on the door signalled to them that the elders in the family would be awake soon, so they better be down in the kitchen, suitably attired. Satnam left first, while she went to a corner to wash the tell-tale bloodstains on the sheet with a jug of water. She dressed and went to the kitchen, and joined her sisters-in-law to go to the village well for their morning ablutions and bath. All the way they teased her, and she blushed.

Thus Mohini spent her days with the ladies, but pining for her husband, and the long spring nights making love; they could never have enough of each other. Like the twinkling of the eye, a month had passed, and her father came to take her home, as was the custom. The summer was upon them when she returned. The bountiful wheat crop brought enthusiasm in the family, and Satnam again began to talk of his ambition to join the army.

Mohini said, "If you have made up your mind then do try to fulfil your aspiration. Talk to your father, and after you get his permission, enrol yourself."

The father put the ball in Mohini's court, saying, "How can I allow him to leave a young bride and go in the army? What if something happens to him?"

Mohini said, "If something has to happen, it will happen anyway, but a man should be allowed to do what he wants in life."

So, a fortnight later, on an auspicious day, Satnam was to set out for Lahore, where enlistment was taking place. Mohini requested him to take her along for she had never been outside the village. Satnam asked his father if he could take her, and he said, "Alright, but take your mother along too, for Mohini should not be left alone, when you go to the army headquarters." There was also the hint that that would take care of any resistance from the mother at Mohini going to Lahore—how simply manipulative the old man was. So, on the appointed day they left for the bus stop outside the village. The village elders advised them not to travel for they had heard news of uprisings in several major cities, but danger is not real until one sees it. They stopped at the bus stop where a couple of buses were parked. In front of one bus on a board near the top was written, 'Chakwal to Amritsar'; on the second was written, 'Chakwal to Lahore', and Mohini realised this was how one knew which bus to board. She had been wondering how they would know which bus to go on. They boarded the one for Lahore, where they reached by evening, and asking directions to the nearest Gurudwara, they arrived there in time for the evening prayers and 'Langar', a meal in the community kitchen. They got accommodation to stay there the night, and in the morning, Satnam left for the army headquarters. When he enrolled, and after they took all his information, his physical tests, which he passed beautifully, he was given a slip and told that he would get a letter when he had to report again. When he was leaving, the officer told him, "We are glad you are joining, we need healthy and brave young men like you," and Satnam was happy.

Walking back to the Gurudwara, he passed by the beautiful bazaars of Lahore, and he was spellbound—such big shops, such a variety of goods, such sparkling garments for women, smart coats and trousers for men, bicycles, radios, gramophones that he had only heard about, and amazing toys—he could not take his eyes off them. He thought how happy his mother and wife would feel when he brought them there the next day; and he would buy them identical gifts with the money he had been quietly saving, and also gifts for his brothers' wives. Lost in his day dream, he suddenly noticed that the shops had started closing down one after the other. He asked a passer-by, who told him, "The Hindu leaders have started a meeting in the market square to protest against the Muslim League's call for a separation of the country in the event of the British leaving. The crowds are sure to become rowdy and then the police will come and do 'Lathi Charge'. You better scurry off unless you want to get hurt."

Satnam was dazed. He did not know what a meeting was and 'protest' was a new word for him—what was there to fear, it was only some people collected together—what harm could they do him? The leaders began their speeches. The first one said, "We have lived for generations with our Muslim brothers, why should we now be told to have separate countries? No village has ever had a Hindu-Muslim quarrel, and why should we be asked to leave our homes of centuries? The Muslim League only wants power for itself, and it is misleading the people. We, Muslims and Hindus of India, have nothing to fear from each other."

"Hindustaaaan", he shouted, and the gathering shouted, "Zindabaaad". Then someone shouted, "Muslim League" and the crowd shouted, "Murdabaad". Then another speaker began to give a more agitated speech. Satnam was both thrilled and terrified; he had never seen anyone speak against anything, in his village; one just accepted what the elders told you. The meeting was swelling in numbers, more slogans were being shouted, and the whole street was full of people. Suddenly, a busload of policemen arrived carrying batons and some carrying guns. The officer had a microphone on which he shouted, "Everyone disperse at once, this is an order. If you do not obey, we will charge upon you. Please disperse at once, do not create unrest in the city, please obey the order." At this, people began to shout louder slogans, they were filled with their cause, and they were shouting out their angst.

Again the officer thundered, "This is an order of the Commissioner of the Police, leave this place at once. I shall count till three—if you do not disperse, then my men will charge."Some men did start to leave, but the leader called them back. "Cowards! Cowards, don't be cowards. We have to fight, fight for our right, for our country; we will face the batons bravely, so that our children live in an undivided Hindustan", even as the officer counted "One, Two, Three, Charge!" Poor Satnam was as though fixed to the ground, and he was also curious to see what a 'charge' was, and that was his undoing. He stood gaping at the running policemen, and the first baton caught him straight on his head. As he ducked in pain and held his face, his left shoulder got the second, the third broke his back as he fell to the ground. Later in the government Hospital the attending doctor wrote in his report, "Brought dead. The cause of death is excessive external and internal bleeding from multiple fractures." A policeman came next morning to take Mohini and her mother-in-law to the hospital, but their world had crashed.

Due to his small connection with the army, his family was contacted quickly. And both his brothers came with their father to receive his body, the mightiest burden for any father anywhere to bear. They cremated him in Lahore, and sobbing, left for their village.

Mohini was too stunned to understand what had befallen her, poor girl. The world was empty suddenly, and so was her life without Satnam. For a week, people congregated to their house almost all day, mourning with the family. The women would repeatedly begin wailing, and the men, mostly elders, would huddle together and try to come to terms with the political situation. They discussed and discussed, but were utterly confused. One elderly man said, "We have to assess the situation as it is, and if it looks like there is going to be a partition of the country, we should make preparations to leave this village and look for a safe place to shift to, where we have some relatives or friends, so that we get help to start life anew."

But another said, "How can we leave the homes of our ancestors and go away? We own our fields, our houses, and we have tilled this land forever; and suddenly we are told to start life like beggars. No, we will not go anywhere."

Then the elderly one said, "I have a suggestion. We have cropped the wheat and taken the money for it, which can sustain us for some time. I suggest we lock up our houses, and taking our gold and money with us, travel to some place in Eastern Punjab or wherever we have relatives who can put us up for some time; then if things remain peaceful, we can return in time for the corn season. It is wise to play safe. Ultimately, everyone makes his own decision."

The women were heard voicing different concerns. One was heard saying, "What will become of Mohini now? If Satnam had a younger brother, he would have married her."

Another woman said,"It is the custom in case there is no unmarried son in the family that a cousin of Satnam can also be asked to take her for a wife. But even that is not so. I'm sure one of his elder brothers will take her as a second wife. Her parents cannot take her back—marrying a daughter once is so difficult, what will they do with her now, such a young widow."

It was actually a very practical custom in the Punjab—where a widow would be automatically taken as a wife, even as a second wife by one of her deceased husband's brothers. Thus they could ensure her sustenance, and that of any children she had, and also the family land and any other share of the departed man would remain in the family; in such cases another wedding was not held—a simple exchange of white sheets between the widow and the brother, with the village being witness was enough. But when Mohini heard this conversation, she was shocked. She knew at once she was never going to get into any alliance. Her marriage to Satnam was forever, and no other man was ever going to touch her. She decided to talk to her mother-in-law and convey her intention.

Night fell and the house was silent as a grave. Mohini felt the world was a grave, and she a walking dead body. As she crouched in a corner of her room, no sleep or any balm was there for her. She wept and then she sobbed, she sobbed and she wept; counting through the long hours for morning to happen, but to what avail? Suddenly, her door opened and there stood Satnam's two brothers, clad in their dhotis, full of arrogance, and their eyes full of lust. The elder one, patting his beard, spoke like a barbarian, "Satnam is gone, and we have all the right on you now. Come, choose which one of us is to mate you now. Would you choose me, with more money. I can buy you new gold bangles every year; or would you choose the younger one, for he is more handsome? But come to us, and we will care for you forever."

Mohini forgot to cover her face, shocked at their insinuations. Her head spun as he took an ominous step forward, saying, "You're no beauty, so don't be coy. Let me sleep with you today and I will see how good you are. Let me taste the juices which made my brother crazy for you—surely there is something in you that makes you so desirable."

As they took two more steps, Mohini sprang like a tigress, and finding the gap between them and the door ran through it, down the stairs, and unbolting the main door, ran out of it. She had to do that for she could not fight them all. This man had the audacity because the whole village would give him the right to ravage her; ostensibly, he would be providing care to his brother's widow, but it would never be acceptable to her, so she had to flee. Run, run as fast as possible, as far as possible, just run. In the silent night, her bare feet made no sound, but there was no other sound either. She suddenly realised she was not being chased any more; the two must not have disclosed their actions to anyone—they must also be sure they would catch her—after all how far could she go? She knew no one outside the village.

She paused to look back, in the dark breezy night, and saw no one; she had left behind the cluster of houses, and saw only the blank fields around her, the stars witness to her plight. She walked to the nearest tree and sat under it to think; where could she go? She knew no place outside the village; but wait, she knew how to get to Lahore. But she knew no one in Lahore. So much better, no one would then trace her, and it may be easy to lose oneself in a big city. Hiding behind trees and pausing behind shrubs, she made her way to the bus stand, and hid behind a huge pile of cow-dung cakes outside the bus driver's house, praying that no one would come here to look for her. Before the sky showed any sign of sunrise, activity started in the driver's house, and soon a man came to clean the bus.Just as the first hint of red showed in the sky, the driver came and started the bus, and honked twice. Soon a few men arrived and began boarding the bus. Mohini could not see the destination from where she hid, but decided to take the first bus, no matter where it went for she was desperate. She trembled at the thought of Satnam's family catching her and taking her back.

The driver shouted, "Anyone for Lahore, the bus is ready to leave."

"Thank God," thought Mohini, and darted out, pulling her 'dupatta' over her face. She sprang aboard the bus, walked to the last corner seat and sat down, even as the bus began to move. Throughout the journey, she prayed, she sobbed, wept silently with tears flowing and wetting her veil, then prayed again. People looked at her with curiousity, but no one approached her, for one could never know if the veiled lady was a Muslim, a Hindu, or even a Sikh. No one could know if she was alone or accompanied by a man. She never got out when the bus stopped for lunch or anywhere else, alighting only when they reached Lahore. The man in the front seat commanded his family, "Hurry up and pick up your bags, we have to rush to the railway station," and immediately Mohini decided to follow them to the railway station, for a train would definitely take her further away from her family. Entering the station, the first train she could see had ' Lahore-to-Abbotabad' printed on all the coaches, and she thought this must be the same way one identified the destination of the train; she was terrified to ask anyone about it. She remembered the only friend she had who lived outside her village—Anjana, who was so rich that she used to come visiting her parents in the village in a motor car. This friend lived in the town of Abbotabad. Anjana was very friendly to Mohini, and spoke to her of her house in Abbotabad, her many servants, and that they had a fleet of buses. " If ever you come to Abbotabad, just ask for the house of the owner of the 'Abbotabad—Amritsar Bus Service' and you will be brought to my house," Anjana had often told her. But Mohini was afraid of the train, as she had never seen one, and did not know how one travelled by it. Again, fear is the basic premise for courage to come alive, and she made her choice. She went and sat on a corner seat again, not even sure where the train would take her—only sure that she had to go, just go.

Anjana

ANJANA RUBBED her eyes in disbelief, blinked and thought, 'Am I where I think I am? Am I hallucinating, or am I seeing a ghost? This trembling, cringing apparition does not belong here; she belongs to a distant place, in my mother's village.' But as Mohini saw the recognition in Anjana's eyes, and tried to say a word she fainted with exhaustion, thirst and hunger. Later, after being fed and washed and given clean clothes, she spoke to Anjana. "Didi I can never go back to the village, you are my only hope; I request you to let me join your numerous servants and remain here, but only if you promise to never let anyone in the village know."

"I shall talk to my husband; he is very helpful to everyone, I am sure he will be able to solve your problem, and please, you are a friend, more like a sister; never talk of being a servant to anyone; God is great, and one day you will be commanding a team of servants, mark my words." said Anjana.

Kartar was tall and fair, a true blood 'Pathan', with robust features and a robust demeanour.His father had had business interests in Kabul, Peshawar, Amritsar and Abbotabad, trading in all sorts of foodstuffs; sourcing dry fruits from Kabul, fabrics and Pashminas from Kashmir, also apples and saffron; wheat, corn and rice and other foodgrains from Amritsar. Being from a very wealthy family, he had studied till his graduation in the Government College in Lahore, where he had learnt from other boys about the transport business. He was always fascinated with motor vehicles, so when his father divided his business and holdings among his four sons, Kartar decided to start a transport service between Peshawar and Amritsar, starting with just two buses, and expanding to a fleet of twelve. Due to his preoccupation with the new business, he was twenty-six when he decided to marry, too old for the times; people predicted he would only catch a widow at that age, but someone found him a match with Anjana, who was sixteen and already been given up as being too old for marriage.

He was wise and mature, a loving husband, and a doting father to their three kids. He was shocked how Mohini could travel up to Abbotabad, and decided it had to be fate. When

Anjana declared they would now have to be responsible for the young widow, he began to think of the best way to help her. He had to talk to her first; and Mohini came to sit in the veranda where he was, shy but confident.

"I am astonished how you could travel all the way to this place and find us, and I believe that it has to be your destiny and ours; and now that God has chosen to place you under our care, we will do our best. I know you are from a good and prosperous family; we will see to it that your dignity and respect is maintained. Now tell me, after running away from your home, though terrified at the time—now that you are at rest, and have had time to think peacefully, what would you like to do? You know the times are bad, the split of the country may be announced at any time, and even survival may become difficult; neither Muslims nor Hindus will take it quietly, and there may be lots of fighting and usurping and even riots. Would you prefer to go back to the safety of your family? I could go personally and apologise for your absence, and settle you back," Kartar said to Mohini. "Never," she retorted.

"Then maybe you could live with your parents," said Kartar.

"No! Even they will force me to go back to my in-laws."

"Then please tell me what do you see for your future. You could live with us forever, you'd be welcome, but sooner or later you'd be discovered; and the right place for a young girl is either at her father's or her husband's home. That is the social structure, and it has always been so."

Mohini spoke courageously, "I have given it plenty of thought. I have studied up to class seven; if somehow I could study three more years and finish Matric, I could get a teaching job, and with some private tuitions and other small jobs, I could earn an honourable living and live independently, without being a burden on anyone."

"Do you know the plight of single women in our society—they are the brunt of so much sarcasm and torture, and even the most virtuous are treated like whores, pardon me using that word—they get no respect."

"I know that. But I will live as an honourable woman, and there will never, never ever be another man in my life. In the worst circumstance, I promise you, I will not kill myself, no. I will kill the person who tries to break my vow, the one to myself, and to my Satnam. My mind is made up; I will live honourably and with Satnam's memory. His blessings are with me always. Whatever may be my situation, if bad times come and I cannot study or work, then I will work as a household maid, no work is less dignified; one's intentions should be dignified. I promise you, I will never give up my honour or dignity, or fall in the eyes of my Father, my Waheguru."

"Ok, give me a day or two to think what best can be done; meanwhile, enjoy your time with your friend. Anjana is such a good soul, I am grateful to God to have her. Also relax, you will have tough times ahead."

Anjana was very keen to keep Mohini with her forever. Having a friend with you always is like being in Paradise. She did try to plan methods to make it possible, but her efforts weren't good enough. The next day, Kartar already had a plan in place. He called Anjana and Mohini and told them, "This is what I have decided to do. Since the future, at least the near future of Abbottabad is uncertain, I plan to shift my family and my vehicles and the transport business temporarily to Amritsar, where we have a nice house too; then I shall see how the political situation changes. After settling everything in Amritsar, I shall take Mohini to Simla, where she will join a boarding school, so that once her fees are paid, she can continue her education uninterrupted. I shall arrange special English tuitions for three months, for in Simla they teach only in English. In three months you will surely catch up. By the time you finish school, Mohini, you will be quite clear about what you want to do for a career, and it is my promise to you, a foster brother's promise, I will support your education till the end. I know you will work hard and do well. No one will be able to trace you in Simla, and even if that happens, the boarding schools are very safe; they will not allow anyone not verified by me to even meet you. I think it should be fine for you."

"Oh, you are too kind. A boarding school will be too costly, I cannot burden you so much," said Mohini.

"Thank God, I can afford the cost. Now that is decided, Anjana, please arrange a reasonably fine wardrobe for this young girl, and quickly too."

Thus, sitting before the principal of St Bede's school, Mohini was enrolled for class eight, and when asked her name, she immediately said, "Kumari, my name is Kumari".

"Please give the complete name," said the principal.

"Kumari Mohan, my surname is Mohan, first name is Kumari, Ma'am," Mohini was ready with her new identity, and Kartar was satisfied.

St Bede's became her home for the next three years; she never left the place. India gained its freedom from British rule, the partition of the country took place, a large chunk of Indian history went by, and Mohini, no, 'Kumari' looked through the school windows for signs of things that she heard were happening. She heard of the trauma the Hindus and Muslims were going through, of the riots, the manslaughter, the lush fields littered with bodies, Hindu and Sikh women jumping into wells, to save their honour from marauding hordes, even heard of Sikh fathers slashing their young daughters' throats to prevent them from falling into Muslim hands and being forcibly converted—but never asked about her mother or father, or her brothers, though she was sure Anjana would know. That life she had left behind, forever. Kartar came to see her once in a year, when classes changed, and at the end of her final Matriculation exams, came and took her home. She came out to an entirely new world, a different India, a new person herself, to a new foster family. Anjana hugged her, and Kumari Mohan hugged the kids affectionately. The intensive convent education had crafted her into a dynamic young lady, with deadly determination, and fierce discipline. She had made three important choices for her life—she would never forget Satnam, no man would ever enter her personal space all her life and she would learn medicine and be a great doctor.

Meena Madhok

THE PREGNANCY progressed, and Anita bloomed into a beautiful mother-to-be. All creation is a miracle, but the creation of a baby is the most awesome. The first few days when you miss a period, one cannot forget the awesome puzzled mania of that week. Hoping and fearing at the same time—could it be a pregnancy, or is it a false alarm? After an agonising wait of two weeks to get the pregnancy test done, the frantic prayers till the report, and the sublime ecstasy when the report is positive. Nothing had prepared Anita for this experience; her brain seemed to be substituted with cotton wool, she felt so lightheaded; the sickly-sweet taste in the mouth, a faint new fragrance in the nostrils, everything smelt and tasted different. A whole month passed in the euphoria, as though she was the first woman ever to have become pregnant. The first tiny kick in the tummy took her breath away—how could the baby do this already? She marvelled at the gradually growing paunch, the odd cravings for food at odd times, and she wept when the first few drops of milk appeared on her breasts, how she loved the tiny creation growing inside her.

She even wanted to enjoy each labour pain, holding Amit's hand as he helped in the delivery, and when the baby gave a hearty cry, Anita wept with joy. Amit showed her the new born baby girl, and Anita felt it was the most precious gem she had ever received, and decided to name her 'Rattna'.

A week later, she prepared to leave the hospital, and Amit said, "You will walk out to a beautiful surprise," and led her to a brand new Fiat car. "My wife and little princess will go home in a new car," he announced. "Later, darling," he said, as he saw the question on her face, "I shall explain later how did I afford it; allow me the pleasure of driving you home now, please."

The next few months Anita was totally wrapped up with her baby, and Amit asked if he could convert her studio into a minor clinic, as she was anyway fully occupied with Rattna, and he would hire a new one when she started to paint again.

Soon, an X-ray machine came in, along with basic surgical equipments and trolleys, and Amit explained he needed them for treating minor fractures or tissue tears, for he wanted to augment his income. Then, one day a lady doctor, Doctor Meena Madhok joined him in the clinic. She would be there all day, while Amit worked with Dr Subrot in the morning and evening. A lot more changed after this.

Anita noticed ladies walking in at the clinic and leaving in some hours, and found that Dr Meena was doing abortions surreptitiously.This shocked her, as it was totally illegal; but Amit said they were never going to be caught, for the women would never divulge; it was as much in their interest as his to keep their abortions secret.

" That's not the point, Amit," said Anita, "what you are doing is illegal, and you have no way to tackle an emergency like haemorrhaging or a drug reaction here should something go wrong. Besides, Meena has no assistant should she take ill suddenly. It is mandatory to have an assistant always; this place is not at all fit for conducting any sort of surgery, your carelessness could be fatal to the patients"

"So where does a woman go with an unwanted pregnancy?" asked Amit, "at least she is getting a professional to help her, otherwise she would go to quacks and untrained midwives, and die of infections. Calm your conscience—we are offering professional healthcare at less than half the price of a hospital, and have had no emergency at all. Meena is good at her job, and I am good at mine. The city is full of joints smaller than ours that do not even have good doctors manning them—we are not the only ones."

All Anita could do was sulk, and even that stopped after some time. As usual, noble thoughts are quickly shelved when the lucre is good. She had never been one with a strong character, had always leaned on Amit, and he had always amply supported her, ever since they were kids. It had been so convenient for her, spared her so many tough decisions she would have made if she was on her own. Despite being honest and righteous in her beliefs, she had lacked the courage of her convictions, and had easily allowed Amit to have his way. She was basically the lazy one, comfortable being a creeper on the trunk of a bigger plant. It was laziness that made her give up her ambition of studying medicine for she evaded the hard work; and though she was a good artist, she never aggressively marketed her work, or followed her career ambitiously. Amit was grossly ambitious, and spared no effort to achieve his ambitions; Anita was simply happy to go along. She was his alter-ego.

Meena, on the other hand, was very ambitious. She knew what she wanted in life and said it unabashed to Anita, "I want to be very successful, famous and rich. Look, I am already buying a car next month, and plan to buy a house in a year. Following that, I plan to have my own big hospital, and I swear, I will achieve it all."

Diwali had just gone by—Rattna's first; and Amit soon announced that he was taking her on their very first trip abroad. Anita was delighted, but surprised when he said they were going to Berlin and a couple of towns nearby, for that was hardly a holiday destination, especially when you went for the first time. But he said the trip was being majorly financed by a surgical equipment manufacturer from there.They were pleased with Amit as he was using a large quantity of their implants.

"Their envelope is way bigger than Dr Saarthi's, but is an envelope all the same," Anita said sarcastically, but Amit shrugged off her remark. His conscience did not prick, and if hers did, she could handle it herself. The trip was very enjoyable; the landscape in so many different shades of green and rows of flowers of all colours formed the landscape of the country, while the sky was the deepest blue. The colours of the pre-winter blossoms, wide open spaces, and the strictly disciplined population, all made their stay very pleasant. Amit was away for three days, for some special surgery training, he said, and on the evening preceding their return, the directors of the company invited them to a grand dinner, and the chairman told her, "You have a dynamic and progressive husband, lucky girl. We look forward to seeing more of him, and hope our partnership proves to be profitable for all of us." This surprised her, but Amit would not divulge much, saying she would come to know when the time came.

That came quite soon. Amit acquired a huge plot of land in a new and upcoming neighbourhood to build his own new hospital, a very ambitious project. Amit was to be chairman, Meena the CEO, and Anita the director for financial operations. The people who had sponsored their foreign trip were the secret financers and partners, but Amit told her this was to remain 'top secret'. She was now his active accomplice.

Miss Mohan

MOHINI JOINED medical college, Kartar supporting her at every step, and studied diligently. She had found her calling, and was happy. She never failed to remember Satnam just as diligently every night; she actually slept with her head on his shoulder, so sensual and caressing in her imagination. She was just brilliant, topping the results each time, making Kartar proud and Anjana happy. Gradually, her personality converted from the soft and shy to a tough and no nonsense lady. The memory of Satnam's brothers never allowed her to trust men, though with time she learnt to keep them at a distance without being offensive. In school, there were only girls, and the atmosphere was one of pampering, but medical college was cut-throat competition. The country was rebuilding itself, and patriotism was high; every student felt he was going to be the best and most dedicated doctor. Even with women she did not tend to be too friendly, mainly to avoid conversations about each others' marital status, which would inevitably happen. She had conveyed to her Principal the facts of her life, for honesty was her main strength, and he had advised her not to divulge it to anyone else, so to everyone she was now simply Miss Mohan.

Four years later, she was a qualified doctor, and was doing her internship at the same hospital where she had studied. Now she came to live with Anjana and Kartar. School was hostel, college was hostel, but now she had to have a place of her own. Anjana and Kartar had adopted her as she too had adopted them—this was the only family for her, the only place she could live at; and after so long, she was not even afraid of being recognized by anyone, for she was a different person now, wearing crisp cotton or silk sarees, and thick black-rimmed glasses, and carrying a huge handbag. Anjana just had her fourth baby, and Miss Mohan doted on her, for it was a baby girl. She also felt the stirrings of motherhood in her heart; she felt how incomplete a woman was without being a mother.

'Well, what cannot be, cannot be.' she said to herself, and dedicated herself to her profession, heart and soul. Over the next months, and years, Anjana and Miss Mohan only grew closer. Now that she was living with them, Miss

Mohan became a part of the family; she began to love the children, to take interest in the kitchen as her friend was weak. She took over a lot of duties of the kids so as to help Anjana. Over time, the kids became so close to her, they wanted to be with her forever. She was so knowledgeable, so wise, they learnt so much from her, which gave them an upper hand with their friends. And she got so much love from them. The love of a family. That she had been craving for, ever since her tragedy. They called her 'Maasi', which means 'mother's sister', and she felt blessed. Kartar assured her that nothing in this scheme of things would ever change. She would always be the closest member of his family, God bless him. Meanwhile, Anjana leaned more and more upon Miss Mohan. She was weak from the last delivery, and the attention required by four growing children, and a loving husband, and the husband's robust social companions—Anjana did not feel up to it all. The graceful Miss Mohan did her best to help the family routine run smoothly, with whatever time she could spare from her hospital duties.

Anjana and Miss Mohan grew close during this period. They were like two women of the same background, sharing their day to day problems, overcoming them, like sisters who do not need words to communicate. Anjana was more and more inclined towards spirituality, and loved to listen to 'Guruvaani' and 'Kirtan'. Whenever possible, she also visited several saints to seek their guidance to understand the scriptures well, and follow them better. She even invited them home to bless her family, including Mohini, as for her she was family; she spent more and more time in chanting and prayer. The wisdom she achieved, she shared with Mohini, who developed a softer side to her persona. They complemented each other, one a science scholar, one a spiritual seeker. Mohini was almost totally a house-maker with Anjana, while she was home; but at the hospital, she was a totally different person. Everyone who came in contact with her simply froze before her cold eyes. Her eyes seemed to have X-ray vision and one felt she could look into one's soul, and read one's mind. But one also felt that here was a person one could depend upon totally; one felt secure in her hands. This lady would do nothing wrong, this is what one felt with her. And if she felt that someone's intentions were not clear, she could pierce your thoughts with the power of her eyes, till you forced yourself to think straight. And when she smiled at you, you felt you had been blessed—she put you totally at ease.

She was doing the OPD duty one day, when the college gardener came in with his wife and a tiny baby, maybe just a day or two old. "We have no children of our own, Madam," he said,"and after eight years of being married, we have adopted this baby boy. Please give him a thorough check-up, and any required treatment if he is deficient." Miss Mohan was as pleased as they were, and while she checked the baby, she felt he was dehydrated.

"How are you feeding him?" she asked.

"We diluted cow's milk with water and fed him with a feeder, but he did not drink much."

"How many days was he with his mother? And why did you get him so soon? He should be fed by his mother for some weeks before you take him."

"Madam, we got him from Beas, so we don't know the mother, and it is most likely that he was not at all fed before we got him." Miss Mohan was surprised.

"Is there an institution in Beas where they help you to adopt babies?"she asked.

"Madam, I thought you would know about Beas. Actually, there is a huge religious centre at Beas, which is an hour's journey from Amritsar, and they have a very large following from all across the world. But there is no railway halt there except for some shuttle trains. So invariably the pilgrims coming to Beas take a train for Amritsar, pull the emergency chain when the train passes by Beas, and get off the train.

"Mostly the train guard looks the other way, but it is mandatory for him to go through the train to find in which coach the chain was pulled, which takes him some minutes.

A lot of unwanted babies are born every day somewhere or other, some to unwed mothers, some out of wedlock, adultery, whatever; sex is the biggest human weakness. Many people who know about this halt at Beas, carry their unwanted babies, and while the guard goes up and down the train, quickly leave the tiny bundle behind a bush, and reboard the train.

"The religious sect in Beas is known for their kindness and generosity, so the people, even though almost killing a new-born baby, hope that someone may find the baby and take it to the centre where it would be assured of a caring and healthy environment. Some people also try to search for such babies, to sell them in a city to childless couples; like we got this baby from one such man. He assured us that he found him as soon as the train left, and that he was crying heartily. Also, he looked weak and parched. Please check him, Madam, and help us to take care of him till he is healthier—he is our only hope of ever having a child."

Miss Mohan was too shocked for words. "How can people be so cruel? What if some animal got to the baby? A baby could simply die if left unattended like that."

"That too happens often—after all, when one abandons one's baby, one cannot ask for insurance."

The gardener said,"Please Madam, if you have seen the baby and written the medicine, can we leave now?"

"Oh yes, and please see me every day for a week so that we can monitor his development. I congratulate you on getting a baby, your own, and wish for him the best of health."

Miss Mohan's mind got no peace after this encounter. The episode persevered through all her activities and all her thoughts. She could not believe what she had heard; and if it was true, then she was not going to allow such cruelty to prevail. Over the next weekend, she boarded a train bound for Delhi, sitting in the ordinary class so as to observe people better, and predictably, more than an hour later, the train ground to a stop. Stepping to the door, she could see a red boundary wall housing a few cottages, though there was no station or platform. She innocently enquired from a passenger why the train had halted there, and he said, "Don't you know, this is where you get off if you wish to visit the Satsang at Beas?"

"But how can I alight when there is no platform?" she asked again. "And how can the train stop if there is no station?"

"Someone always pulls the chain and the train stops, even the engine driver respects the Satsang visitors. Come, I can help you to alight. If you have to go to the Satsang, you just walk across to the gate. It is always open for visitors."

"But if the train moves while I am getting off, what will I do?" she said again.

"No, the train will not move till the guard has found the place where the chain was pulled, and look, people are already walking across towards the place." So with the help of this unknown traveller, she got off the train and walked towards the red wall. She was welcomed at the gate and asked if she was alone. "Yes, I have come alone," she said to the man at the gate."Is Babaji available in the Ashram, and can I meet him?"

"Babaji is in the Ashram, but you can rest a little and eat something in the 'Langar' before you greet him; that is his instruction for every visitor."

The man, a 'Sewadar' guided her towards a hall where she could keep her small bag, for she had brought along a change of clothes as she intended to stay overnight, and go around doing some furtive investigations; she was allotted a cupboard to keep the bag, and told to return the key when she left. After she freshened up, she was led to the 'Langar hall' where they served a simple lunch of dal and roti along with hot sweet tea. Then she was told to rest in a hall along with other women, for Babaji would be available for 'Darshan' only in the evening. Miss Mohan spent the time walking around the Ashram, admiring the cleanliness, and the beautiful patches of flowers and green lawns. She sat beside a lady who was resting near the Langar Hall, for she was a part of the team who prepared Langar. Getting into a conversation with her, she started simply with, "You are fortunate to be serving Babaji, one should touch your feet and take your blessings."

"The blessings are all from Babaji, we are too small. I am grateful Babaji has given me place at his feet, and I have a cover over my head, security, and food to eat; otherwise, I would be nowhere," said Seeto, for that was her name.

"Since when are you here, and where is your family?" asked Miss Mohan. "I lost my family in the riots, and I was about to jump before a train to end my life, when someone saved me and brought me before Babaji. Babaji told me I had no right to take my life, and placing his hand on my head blessed me with peace. Since then, he has allotted to me this duty of preparing Langar, and now my life is worthy again."

Miss Mohan carried the conversation further slowly, pretending to be from a modest, middle class family, looking for peace for her soul and meaning for her life; gradually finding out the routines at the Ashram, the various people and their domains of authority, the method of maintaining the security of the place, the type of visitors, everything. She meandered the conversation towards the presence of single women like her, and the presence of orphaned children.

"Yes," said Seeto, "there are several motherless children here, and they are lovingly brought up by Babaji and all the Sewadars. They are well fed, and sent to school, and if they have merit, they are sent to college. Babaji has a lot of influence in industry and government, so he arranges jobs for the boys; and the girls are educated till the Matric and then married into good households, which Babaji chooses."

"Is it true that Babaji helps childless couples to adopt abandoned children, thus helping both the baby and the couple?" "Yes he does when he is sure of the people being kind and God-fearing. But they have to be staunch followers of his sect. Otherwise, he keeps them in the Ashram and they are brought up to live according to his teachings, and taught to be totally loyal to him."

"I have heard that a lot of abandoned children are brought in every month, for people know that if they are brought here, they are assured of food and care, so people abandon their unwanted children near the Ashram, maintaining some sort of kindness in their absolute cruelty."

"Previously two or three babies would be brought in every month, mostly found near the railway track, but now we get a baby in a month, or sometimes two, poor things. I have seen a couple of mauled babies brought in, who could not be saved.Then Babaji prayed for their souls and asked them to be washed and wrapped in white fabric, and confined to the river Beas. It was very sad."

"Does no one try to catch the people who leave them there?" Seeto sighed, " Only God can see you when you sin, and He never misses, though man may try to hide his sins from everyone."

So that was that, this hideous fact was a sad truth. Anyway, Miss Mohan met Babaji at the evening Satsang, stayed on the night and met him again in the morning, too. While blessing her, he said, "I hope you found what you came here to see. You are a good soul, and you are going to rise to unimaginable heights in your life, trust in God. Forget your past, only work hard; accept what God gives you. Do not ask for what is not yours in life, it will not bring you happiness. I bless you as a father would his daughter." And thanking him, she returned to Amritsar.

The superitendent of police

MISS MOHAN could not rest; her mind and soul could not accept this whole trauma about unwanted babies—mothers giving them birth, only to throw them away to find their fate? She definitely held the mothers responsible for the babies—a woman should choose the right way in life. But again, she pondered, what about the women who were compromised, or even raped, who were not willing participants in their pregnancies, but still had no way to do away with them either? Oh God! This trauma occupied her mind totally, and some days later she went to see the superitendent of police. She narrated to him all that she had comprehended, but he already knew everything.

"Then how come you have done nothing about it?" she asked.

"Well, we did," he replied. "We became aware that people were scavenging for babies, and began a patrol to deter the people from abandoning their babies in that particular area; but it backfired. More people began to leave babies there, conscious that whether the Satsang people found them, or the police found them, they would at least live. So we stopped that programme at once. Sometimes we have to lose the fight, or just give up—we don't always win, Miss Mohan." Her heart sank and tears flooded her eyes; she actually had to take off her spectacles and use a handkerchief, perhaps for the first time ever.

The SP consoled her, "We never found it alarming; you are too emotional. Abandoning, even killing unwanted daughters at birth has gone on for centuries in Punjab; people have become quite used to it. If a relative is told that his cousin or someone had a stillbirth, they immediately know that it must have been a girl child, who must have been done away with. Have you not heard the story about the mother of Maharaja Ranjit Singh?"

"No," said Miss Mohan, "Please tell me."

"Sure. There was this saint, a follower of the Sikh religion and one of its chief missionaries, Sant Karam Singh of Hauti Mardan, which is now in Pakistan. Once while travelling, he stopped at a village for the night, and the Sarpanch of the village requested him to have the evening meal with his family, as is the custom when saints and preachers cross your village. It is auspicious to serve the pious people and get their blessings. Well, the Sant came in and spoke about Guruvaani, and said prayers; then the family served him the meal. Just as he dipped his hand into the first morsel, he stopped. 'This meal I cannot eat; you people are sinners, you have committed a very serious crime right here, in this house; and I cannot eat the food offered by sinners.' And he got up to leave. The family prayed and cajoled, 'We assure you we abide by the teachings of the Guru Granth Sahib; we say all the prayers, and donate in the Gurudwara, we have done no criminal activity; please do not leave without eating, for we will suffer the wrath of a saint if you do so.' But Santji got up to leave. Just then the lady of the house spoke, 'We did commit a crime—everybody does it—you are wise, and your perception is Godly; three days ago our daughter-in-law gave birth to a girl, and we duly buried her in a corner of the courtyard, that is all. We have done nothing criminal. But if you believe so, we will ask your pardon, and the pardon of Guruji, and not do so in future.'

'Where,' he bellowed, 'where have you buried the child? Open the place at once.' The family quickly opened the new grave, and there was the baby, miraculously alive with her eyes wide open, sucking her thumb. Santji bowed before her and told them to take her out and feed her at once. Later, when she was fed and washed and brought before Santji, he looked at her and said, 'Do you know who she is? She will give birth to the future king of Punjab, who will shine and be the pride of the Sikhs forever. Sikh faith forbids discrimination between male and female at any stage. Sikh women can be priests , and can fight wars shoulder to shoulder with the Sikh men, never forget that. Also, always remember the most important dictat of Guru Gobind Singh—whichever Sikh either kills a daughter, or partakes of her wealth, is ousted as a 'Tankhaiya'. Of the five major commands given by Guruji, the second most important is the Sikh law against female discrimination.' Well that girl Santji saved, when she grew up and was married, gave birth to the child who went on to become Maharaja Ranjit Singh, the Lion Of Punjab, and none can compare with his valour or his generosity for his contributions to the 'Guru Ghar'. If Santji had not gone there, that baby girl would have soon died. That's the way it's been in the Punjab for generations. Still Madam, I will address this problem and see if something can be done to improve the situation. Honestly Madam, we are trained to fight all anti-social activity, but we are also trained to remain within our powers, and then we are helpless. I promise you my best co-operation and wish you peace of mind."

"Thank you Sir, I have used a lot of your valuable time, I hope I can be of use to you sometime too, and may God bless you." and Miss Mohan left.

Rattna

IT WAS going to be Rattna's first birthday, and Anita was in a flurry of activity. Her bundle of joy was so beautiful, she never tired of admiring her; she could not believe that she had given birth to such a pretty child. She took delicate little steps, her voice was so soft, and her touch simply divine. Anita felt totally fulfilled as a woman with this baby around, and she centered her life around her; almost all her thoughts, wishes, aspirations and hopes ultimately centred on Rattna. She made a million plans for her angel's birthday. One day she wished to have a smashing party; the next day she wished to share the day with poor children instead, and the next she would want to have a quiet trip to a place of pilgrimage; again she would begin to plan a party; she was utterly confused. But Amit resolved the issue by announcing that they would have the foundation laying ceremony of their hospital on Rattna's birthday, and there would be a 'havan' to pray for Rattna's prosperous and healthy life, and for the success of their venture. He had decided to invite a minister, and even have the event covered by the press. Anita felt happy for Amit—he was getting close to fulfilling his dream, and she felt proud too. The following year, Amit was busy with the building of the hospital, ordering the equipments, arranging staff, certificates and licenses, too many things, and Anita devoted all her time to Rattna.

The mother and daughter were inseparable. Even while sleeping, they would stretch out and feel each other, they were so close. More so because Rattna saw very little of her father. When Anita went back to her painting, she seemed to be putting the theme of mother and daughter on canvas all the time—she would draw something and then draw a miniature of it again, and the syringe in the corner curled up in a big smile. Amit was obviously busy with work and the construction of the hospital, and a whole year seemed to just fly by in a jiffy. Rattna began going to play school by the time the hospital took final shape; just as well, for now Anita would be required to pool in her time at the hospital. "AMAN NURSING HOME AND RECOVERY CENTRE" was opened on the eve of India's Independence Day, by no less than the Home Minister of the country. It was good planning, for after orthopaedic treatment, the next treatment to follow-up is physiotherapy, and the Recovery Centre catered to that need perfectly. It also made sure that there was never a dearth of patients at the hospital.

So, it came about that Rattna joined a very good school and was very happy, and Anita joined the Nursing Home, in her capacity as Director, Financial Operations. Both Amit and Anita were equally proud of the new venture—on the Medical Scene they had now arrived—at least Amit had arrived. His identity was established, as a surgeon with a fully equipped hospital of his own. It was a really well conceptualized and planned place; they had two well equipped Operation Theatres, a whole section for Maternity and Gynaecological care with a separate OT and two Labour Rooms, a Nursery for new born babies, again with all facilities, and a minor OT, too. Dr Meena Madhok was more than satisfied—her dream had been realized. The Rehabilitation Centre astounded everyone; no hospital in the region had anything like that. Dr Subrot also complimented Amit, saying, "You have shown great vision, Amit. Your set-up is already ten years into the future; you will surely gain a march over all of us, I can see most orthopaedics referring to your Rehab, clever guy."

"Was there a hint of envy in that?" wondered Amit, with glee. Anita was alone when he confided that it was all planned by those German partners."If they are our partners, why did they not attend the opening ceremony, and why do we never see them?" said Anita.

"Sh...!" said Amit, "Don't ever mention them for they are not legally allowed to invest in India, or be our partners. But Europe is way ahead of us and they have helped us get the latest machinery and know-how, so that we have an edge over all others. The investments come in finding leaks in our laws, like under-invoicing of equipment which we import legally with a license from the Health Ministry, and of the implants and Surgical sutures and several such stuff. Many other ways to evade the laws, you'll learn as you work along, Madam Director."

"But what do they gain?"

"They get a market for their products, they have a presence in the country, and they already have a foothold when the country opens up its imports, as should happen sooner or later; and, their part of the profits reach them regularly."

"How?" asked Anita.

"Hm.. not all in one day.... "And Meena Madhok?"

"Yes, and Meena Madhok".

The nursing home was quite big and modern by the general standard of the day; there were six consulting rooms on the ground floor, with lines of benches for waiting patients. Amit had enrolled a number of top doctors of the city to work at his hospital, giving them consulting rooms for two hours each, by rotation, and if they took in in-patients, then they got good nursing care at his place too. The ground floor also flaunted the 'Rehabilitation Centre', actually the physiotherapy room, the first in the city. This part of the convalescence process had not been practised much before, it was quite a radical feature. People learnt for the first time that post-operative patients could recover so much faster with physiotherapy, and that so many crippling symptoms could be treated with physiotherapy alone, like 'frozen shoulder', or cervical spondylitis. This hall was the pride of the nursing home, and Amit had hired the best therapists he could from across the country, and also done a short course himself to be able to guide them better. The equipment also was world class. He made a point when he said 'diathermy' instead of 'fomentation with a hot water bottle'. As expected, loads of orthopaedics and doctors from other specialities were soon referring their patients to him. Dr Meena and Anita both complimented him on his foresight.

The first floor gave an impression of vastness. It seemed to be huge, like a very big hospital. There was a small waiting lobby for relatives of in-patients. It was coloured a cheerful pink, instead of the total white elsewhere, and had magazines strewn around, and also a water cooler for drinking water.

Behind the lobby there were the shared rooms, in which there were four patients each, their beds divided by curtains, having a common bathroom and toilet; their companions and relatives had a bench each to sleep at night. There were ten of these rooms on the first floor. Also on the first floor was a Children's Ward with five single rooms, and five double sharing rooms, that had two patients in each room. Then there were twenty special rooms, non air-conditioned, and ten special rooms, air-conditioned. There was a nursing station outside the General ward, the Children's ward, the Non A/c special ward, and the A/c special ward; all well equipped with emergency equipment and medicines, and manned by well trained nurses. Anita would be at the nursing home till 2 pm, and then rush home to Rattna before she could miss her returning from school.

Rattna was very smart too; she could sense that her mother had been away, and could read the flurry of thoughts racing through Anita's mind—the totally relaxed, benign fairy had changed. Now Rattna wanted to protect her. Rattna's thermometer for deciphering the emotional index of her mother was much more sensitive than Anita's. What a bond they shared, where thoughts and emotions were wordlessly exchanged, and automatically they leaned on each other. When Anita got up to call the servant, Rattna was already calling out; when she asked her child what she would like to eat, Rattna asked for exactly what Anita had planned to serve; when it was study time, the child was perfectly tuned into study—reading, writing, learning, all was done amazingly fast; and each night Rattna prayed as hard to God for her mother's health and happiness, as did Anita for her baby. Rattna made few friends, and those were very sensitive and helpful children. She actually had the best friend in her mother, who was also her confidante. But Anita would never have the luxury of having one. She would toss her secrets around her own brain, debate all possibilities herself, and often cover them with a shell to contain them permanently.

Her work at the hospital took more and more energy to fulfil. Handling the finances was not as easy as it looked. The number of Medical Representatives visiting the doctors, ostensibly to update them about the latest products of their companies, often outnumbered the number of patients, and Anita could not understand why doctors spent so much time with them. The cloud cleared when the 'envelopes' started coming in. Speaking to one of the med-reps, she learnt of the system where the doctors were rewarded for each injection, capsule and pill that they prescribed of a particular brand of medicine. She wondered how they could do it, and the young man told her, "Ma'am, we have a parallel team of 'marketing research' working on it. They concur with the records of the chemists, and calculate what is due to each doctor, which is paid in cash every month. Alarmed, she asked him, "Is it worth so much work and manpower?"

"Of course, ma'am, the amount of money going to the doctors almost equals the money going to the pharmaceutical company—they are very big amounts. The costlier the medicine, the bigger the cut." In her capacity as the Financial Director, she was privy to such information, but it caused terrible storms in her brain, and these she would have to learn to deal with, for after all, she was benefitting too.

Her mind was in a turmoil thinking of Rattna's future. Seeing both her parents working at the hospital, she was most likely to aspire for a medical career, which Anita was determined to avoid. Half her waking night she prayed Rattna would make a better career choice, and the other half she thought 'which one, and how?'She wouldn't like her to be an artist either.Artists, she felt now, were simply scavengers from the riff raff that spilt over from the experiments of a quickly growing society—short-lived fillers in the long game of life. The evolving of a true artist consumed almost all of a person's being. His vision, his conflicts, slowly evolving growth, flowering maturity, struggles with both his medium, his family and society was too much hard work with not much success. No, Ratna would do something else; something which complemented her sensitive nature, her soft mannerisms, and delicate behaviour. Maybe a teacher's job would suit her best.She would gradually doze off. In her mind, she had begun to be convinced that Rattna should be kept away from the working of the hospital, the noble medical profession had an ignoble underbelly, and dear delicate Rattna was too sincere. "Oh God, what will I do?"Anita continued to wrack her brains.

Rattna, on the other hand, wondered what had happened to her darling mother; the soft, snuggling, hugging, peaceful, whispering, warm lady had changed into a restless soul, who was never peaceful now, and this had happened ever since she began going to the hospital. 'Maybe she had to work too hard; maybe she could not bear to see the suffering of the patients', she kept thinking. It is unbelievable how deeply small kids can fathom the feelings and emotions of their parents, and how vast is their imagination in trying to find reasons for their behaviour. She felt closer than ever to her mother, and embraced her often, as if to keep out her troubles and reassure her.

But Anita's troubles only grew. Checking out the X-ray rooms, she found the technicians doing two X-rays of some fracture patients, which she could not understand; to her it was a waste of costly X-ray films, and she took it up with them. They did not reply, and said it was procedure, but it did seem fishy. She decided to keep her eyes open. She thought maybe it was some pilferage happening. Soon the mystery was cracked. She found to her dismay that it was a very big racket. Everyone was involved. What was happening was that whenever a new patient came in for a consultation, the consulting doctor would casually ask a simple question, "What do you do, sir?" or with a lady, "What does your husband do?" or "What does your father do?" Guessing the financial status of the person, for example, people in business, exporters, professionals, those financially better off than most, they would make an innocuous mark on the prescription, something like a dot in a corner, which could be understood to have been made accidently by the pen rubbing across the page by the unsuspecting patient, but differently by the hospital staff.

From then on, that patient would be on a different level of treatment from other less affluent people. He would be asked to go for unnecessary investigations, prescribed costlier medicines, and even advised surgery where it was not necessary. For instance, in case of a fracture in the leg, if the patient was likely to recover in a month if his leg was put in a plaster cast, he would still be advised to go in for surgery, and to strengthen their case for surgery, an X-ray of someone else, collected from the 'stock' maintained by the technicians, which would be showing a complex fracture, would be printed with the name of the patient. When they were taking out two copies of the X-rays, one was named and the other kept blank where the name should be. So the X-Ray was used, printing the blank portion with the new patient's name and new date, and even if the patient went to consult more doctors, seeing the 'doctored' X-ray, they would all advise surgery, so back the patient would come. Whereas the plaster cast would have cost him a few hundred rupees, the operation would cost him several thousand, spelling that much more business for the hospital. If by chance, someone did repeat the X-ray elsewhere, and the discrepancy was discovered, they were told simply,"It is a rare mistake, there must have been a mix-up due to similar names or something. And don't worry, when we do any surgery, we repeat the X-ray just before starting, to be sure, so be assured you would never have been unnecessarily operated upon." And they were believed, for a sick person trusts doctors more than God.

Each new revelation, each new turmoil in Anita's mind, never went unnoticed by little Rattna, who worried harder and prayed harder. She was more sensitive than a grown-up.For instance, Anita's mother never found anything amiss; she actually felt happy and proud of their improving finances. But who can fathom the pure souls of little children who can look into your soul with their eyes shut, God bless them. Rattna noticed that her mother almost never touched the easel any more, and if she did, she simply drew syringes—some big, some small, some crooked even, but hardly much else; and she sat before her board staring at the centre, where there was nothing. Then Rattna just hugged her from behind, and kissed her moist eyes, struggling to find why it was hard for Anita to laugh, and what she could do to help.

Ranee

MISS MOHAN was a kind and good doctor, and gradually became very popular in the hospital, so that when the Dean requested her to continue with them after her internship, she gladly agreed. After so many years, she now felt settled in life—no more insecurity for the future, no fears from the past, a pleasant family which was now totally her own, beautiful children, a close dear friend, and in Kartar, a caring elder brother. But often at night, Satnam was back in her memories, giving a sweet throbbing pain in her bosom, creating all the desires that she had learnt to suppress. Then she fantasized, and made believe that she was with Satnam, and her own family, with children and their own house. Then she drowned her dreams with her tears and taking God's name she slept, and awoke in the morning, Miss

Mohan, the doctor. The dream was her private little heaven, that she visited sometimes, and felt happy; though she knew that it was never to be. The knowledge that there were so many unwanted children needing help, and that so many people were quietly adopting babies and filling an important part of their lives by bringing them up, did create a stirring of desire in her heart sometimes.

She thanked God for filling up her life with so much work, and thanked Kartar for all he had done to make her life so meaningful. A passing remark that Kartar made to his elder son made her think of studying further and progressing in her career.

He had said, "As you are crossing your class eight, I want you to get more serious about your studies. You can try to become a doctor like your maasi, or an architect, or lawyer; I can afford your studies to any extent. It is both lucrative and prestigious to be a professional nowadays. In my days, a graduation was a very high qualification, but now, people are aspiring for much higher degrees. You can even sit for the IAS exam and be a part of the government, if you do well. The sky is the limit, son, and you are lucky to have your parents supporting you."

After she discussed it with her Dean at the college, whom, after Kartar, she looked upon as her mentor, he was glad she spoke about it.

"It was already on my mind to talk to you about it. The IAS exam selects candidates for the different courses to train able persons for the administrative services. Any one who is a graduate or more qualified can apply and compete in the exams, and the few who are selected are trained by the government agencies for different departments, and appointed to different ministries and states. I am sure you will succeed in the competition, and being a single woman, for once will be a benefit. Most women do not apply because they are not prepared to leave the security and social standing of their families to accept postings to distant places, but to you it will be an empowerment, and applying your intelligent mind to your work, you will surely be a success. Besides, doctors do only good, wherever they are."

She then spoke to Kartar and Anjana, who both supported her, Anjana hoping that she would not have to leave them. Thus Miss Mohan was launched on the next leg of her journey through life, and within months she stood proudly before her Dean with a great result. He congratulated her and told her to start packing for her training at the special centre in Mussoorie, near Dehradun. Kartar was proud, and threw a party, boasting to all,"I am so proud. My sister has achieved what no one among my family or circle of friends has done. I am very happy today, and I hope to be around when she becomes famous, and brings fame to our country."

Like a whirlwind her next few days passed; everyone seemed to know her wherever she went; people whispered to each other, "This is the first lady from our city to be chosen for the IAS you know." Some newspapers came for interviews, and printed her photographs, but she was focused on the work she was doing and would have to do. The period of training too went by fast, for she was a quick and focused learner, had no social pretences, and wasted no time. Home for a vacation, she found Anjana very unhappy, and Kartar quite upset. Anjana was pregnant with her fifth child, and was not physically strong enough for it. There was already so much work in the house—the children were growing, and so were their needs, and Anjana herself was not in her prime any more. She wept before her friend, "I was always insisting that I cannot bear another child, but he would not listen. When he has had drinks—it is impossible to refuse him sex, and see what I have to go through." "But what about those condoms I got for you,"asked Miss Mohan.

"Those too he has to use, not me. And he refuses, always promising to start the next time. Women are meant to just do what is ordered, and die—we cannot choose."

"Oh, come now; it will not be so bad. I'll get you lots of tonics for building your strength, and calcium for building your bones; the few months will fly, and we'll have a bonny new baby here; then you'll quickly forget your trauma."

"And who will bring up this bonny baby? It is a twenty-four hour job, I am really not up to it. Don't you doctors have any method of stopping this pregnancy now? Some medicine? Anything?"

"Be brave, Anjana," said Miss Mohan, "We are all there with you; you know I will always be by your side." But Anjana could not be consoled. She simply did not want to have another baby, period. Asked about Kartar, she said that he was least concerned; he was not enthusiastic like he used to be before; actually he was quite indifferent, as though it was only Anjana's baby and not his. Miss Mohan helped and consoled as much as she could, but her focus and attention was on her exams, which she had to prepare for in a month's time.

As usual, she breezed through them, and back home with Anjana, hugged her whenever she was upset, and tried to help all the time. One sunny afternoon, Anjana lay in bed, obviously in pain, while Miss Mohan cajoled her to come out and sit in the sun, for it would do her good. She even rubbed her legs, while Anjana only sighed. Miss Mohan shared a most unusual thought with her friend. "Please forgive me if you feel upset, but I need to say something to you, and if it upsets you, simply turn your face away, and we shall both forget this conversation forever, and I shall be saved any embarrassment for being presumptive. Is it possible, darling, that I may adopt the baby you are carrying, and bring it up and be its mother, whatever it may be, a son or a daughter? Our love should be strong enough to make a decision, whichever way. I share with you for the first time my craving to have my own child who will call me 'Mother', but only if it does not upset you. Otherwise, I am quite content with my life—you and Kartar have done enough to make my life meaningful and also successful."

Anjana heard her out, and only stared at the ceiling, neither answered, nor looked away. Miss Mohan left her alone, hoping she had not overstepped her space. Anjana was shocked. Shocked to know that her friend had all the cravings and feelings of an average woman, but had never let anyone know; also that she could be coveting the baby as much as Anjana was regretting having conceived it. Miss Mohan's demeanour had been quite deceptive. She made Anjana feel that she was living, thinking and evolving as a man would have, never letting her know of her womanly feelings. She spoke to Kartar in the morning about the conversation, and was surprised that he was actually happy to gift their baby to Miss Mohan. He said that he cared for her and now even loved her as a younger sister, and would be very glad to make her happy; and also that it didn't matter much who brought up the baby, for it was going to be in the same house anyway.

"In fact, Mohini will certainly care more and perhaps educate the baby better than us too." Then he called in Miss Mohan and said to her, "After ages my dear sister has asked her poor brother for something. It will be my pleasure to put our newborn baby into your arms, to be all yours, that's the least your brother can do. And I promise you my word will not change, whether the baby is a boy or a girl—just pray that we have a healthy baby, whose proud mother will be the great Miss Mohan." For the first time, Mohini let her tears flow, and for the first time Kartar took her in a filial embrace, and patted her head in a blessing; and Anjana wept too, with mixed feelings.

She gave birth to a baby girl, and congratulated Mohini. "Congratulations dear, God has blessed you with a tiny daughter, the most beautiful ever seen. She has a Pathan's cream and peaches complexion, and sharp features. God bless you, and your baby. What do you wish to name her?" And Miss Mohan took the baby in her arms and kissed her forehead, and said, "I shall call her 'Ranee', my queen, and the queen of all I survey." Ranee seemed to smile too, and the happy scene was celebrated by Kartar by passing around a box of sweets, and telling the nurse, "This is my sister's daughter, bless her, and spread the word around that Miss Mohan is not alone in life—she has a child, a daughter named Ranee." It was decided that the baby was not to be separated from Anjana till she was being breast-fed, and till that time, Miss Mohan would finish her training at the IAS institute. Three months later, she was back, a post-graduate IAS officer, appointed to be a medical officer at Dhanbad, a city of coal mines in Bihar. She was to be allotted a bungalow to live in, three domestic servants and a chauffeur driven car at her disposal, with the first promotion already granted due to her superb performance at the training institute.

"Didn't I tell you once that you will be having dozens of servants one day," said Anjana, both happy and perturbed, for now, Miss Mohan would have to leave them.

But Kartar said, "Yes she will go away with Ranee, but look, we will all have a second home in Dhanbad, where we can go for vacations, and be proud of Miss Mohan."

Mohini felt fulfilled like she had never felt before. She had her own baby, and now would have her own house. She suddenly felt how great it was to have a home of one's own.

Ranee was slowly weaned from her mother's breast, and with a lot of preparation, Miss Mohan left for her new posting, travelling first class in the train, with Kartar duly travelling with her to settle her in her new job and new surroundings, helping her with Ranee during the journey, fulfilling the responsibility he took on years ago. They chugged through the long journey, passing through green areas and arid ones, famous towns and rivers, moistening their faces against the afternoon heat, peering through the window to get some evening breeze, but inhaling the sooty smoke of the steam engine, Kartar running out at every station to fill water in their earthen *Suraahi* (pitcher). They reached the small station at Dhanbad to be received by a junior officer and a domestic servant, and by the vacant barren scenery of the scantily populated town. They thought they had come to a desert, there was hardly any greenery. They were taken to Miss Mohan's appointed house in a small car called 'Baby Hindustan' by its manufacturers, through a narrow road, till they reached a cluster of houses, big and small, with a Badminton Court gleaming in the bright sun, somewhere in the centre of the colony, with a hedge of frayed and wilting shrubs. Miss Mohan's house was small, with four rooms and a tiny veranda, a small courtyard behind, and space for a car to be parked in front, without any shade. Kartar was pleased. The furniture was not as good as they had at home, but it was adequate, the kitchen was large and airy, and the domestic helps were already waiting. The next morning, he accompanied her to her office, where she was given charge of her duties. After spending a couple of days helping the staff to learn about Ranee's schedules and care, he took the train back to Amritsar. Before leaving he also threw a dinner for her immediate colleagues, like a true Punjabi. Seeing him off at the station, for the first time perhaps in her life, Miss Mohan felt a pang at the parting, and putting her head down, she cried. She wept remembering the last few years she had basked in the security she enjoyed with him, wept like a bride weeps when leaving her father's house.

Dhanbad

DHANBAD WAS a very small town, near the Damodar river, and owed its existence to the wealth of millions of tons of coal in the belly of the otherwise vacant countryside, having been discovered almost a century ago, that continued to be mined deeper and deeper into the earth's depths, as better and better equipment became available. There was hardly any greenery. Though the area was not arid, but because the earth's belly was pouring out the lucrative coal, nobody did any agriculture. People were not very diverse, the population consisting of some major business families, who mainly owned the small and big coal mines; some Britishers who stayed back after independence to follow their passion of teaching and missionary work; some traders of grocery and other stuff needed in every household; some government servants, for a town of such wealth had to be looked after by the state, and the mine workers who made up the major part of the population. Almost all of them were migrants, and all were very poor. There were very few doctors in the town, but the government had appointed some to take care of the health of the mine workers, since Dhanbad had been appointed as the Headquarters for the Health Department for miners, like Miss Mohan and a few others. She adjusted soon to the mostly brown and parched faces at the mines she attended the clinics at. Coming from north India, though she herself had a similar complexion, it hurt her to see how malnourished they all were. The clinics were badly maintained, the equipment and medicines totally inadequate; even bandages and gauze took several reminders to acquire. She was aghast to see women readily tearing up their sarees, anticipating the lack of bandages. In a place like a coalmine, small and big abrasions were common, considering that the workers dealt with rubble falling from all directions all the time, and not being able to give them first aid made Miss Mohan seethe in anger.

Though she had a sensitive heart, Miss Mohan acted upon the commands of her head. She decided she was going to make a big difference to this town of Dhanbad. She was getting fulfilment in her life here. She had, at last, a home of her own, a workplace of her own, an identity as an officer, and a child of her own. She was going to be worthy of the responsibility she had taken upon herself. She smiled at the joy of her life, little Ranee, whom she kissed on her forehead in blessing every time she held her in her arms, her large mouth covering the whole of the baby's tiny forehead. While she was home, she did all the baby's chores herself, trusting the help only when she was away at the clinic. She not only fed Ranee herself, she washed the bowl to make sure of the hygiene too, cooked fresh whatever had to be fed, and lovingly spooned every tiny morsel into her mouth, singing God's blessings all the while. The beautiful baby with the rose-petal complexion, brought happiness to her mother whatever she did, and the mother was paranoid leaving her alone with the domestics. She would tell all the neighbours to keep looking in on her when she was at work. In that area, she was the only woman going out to work—mostly the men officers were working and the wives were home. Thus, Ranee became the apple of everyone's eye, and enjoyed all the attention and love.

Gradually, Miss Mohan did make improvements in the medical care of the miners. She wrote and wrote, made personal visits to the headquarters, took on the higher officers, and made sure she had ample first-aid equipment in her clinic, had enough antibiotics too. This was tough, for the owners of the mines did not think the workers deserved costly antibiotics; they were used to them working till they could, and simply rest a couple of days when they almost dropped with fever, and report back sick and feverish, fearing a deduction in their pay.

She called a meeting of the managers and owners and explained, while putting figures on the blackboard, "Gentlemen," she said, "I request you to rise above the feudal mindset and think clearly. Even though I believe the mine workers deserve the best treatment medically on human grounds, I can convince you that it is bad business sense if you do not invest in their medicare. For instance, an average worker who gets sick once in a month and is not treated properly, takes two days off, and forces himself to work while still sick or convalescing for the next, say, six days. Those six days, though present at the colliery, he cannot give more than fifty percent of his potential output—it is physically not possible. Other workers understand, so they are sensitive to him. So you pay six days salary for about three days of work. Next, his working in this condition spreads his infection to another dozen workers around him, and when they fall ill, again it is the same count. And, when an infection has not been properly treated, it recurs soon, and the man may be down again with the same illness in less than a month, resulting in so many man-hours lost. But, if treated properly with the appropriate medicines, he may not fall ill for a long time, giving benefit to both the company and the worker. Healthy workers can give you many more years of productivity, while also saving your retirement pensions. Please do not omit the loyalty you will be earning. Also, our government is committed to socialist policies, and is soon going to make an Insurance Scheme for employees mandatory. Consider the loss if you have to pay higher insurance due to consecutive illnesses of workers. It is thus in the interest of the workers, and even more so in the interest of the bosses to increase the spending on the healthcare of the employees. I can assure you, if you co-operate, I could take up a stand for you and convince the government to allow you to charge higher prices for your coal, I will go all the way to help you with that. That is my promise. Please note, you have access to government's help, and you can tap the market for profits, but these poor workers have only you to look up to."

In some time, she did win her case, and facilities improved, and with it the condition of the workers. Her efforts earned her the promotion to the office of the CMO (Chief Medical Officer). She attributed it to Ranee's presence in her life. Everything good in her life was because of Ranee; she really was the princess of her home. She got her the best of everything and still felt she could do more; she doted on her and never let her out of her sight when at home. She cross questioned the help about simple things like her lunch and evening glass of milk till she was a hundred times sure Ranee had been fed the way she had instructed. It was almost an obsession. Sometimes she felt that Satnam had sneaked out of her life, and now Ranee was to be her only companion, only relative and friend for the rest of her life. In fact, Satnam was relieved of his previous role, that of her lover in her fantasies and memory—he was now her constant friend and guide. She seemed to be always consulting him, seeking his approval, sharing her happiness with him, as also her pride in her own progress. And how could she forget Anjana and Kartar, who had made this happiness possible for her? She wrote to them regularly, and they wrote back, all three longing to be together again.

Little Ranee loved only Miss Mohan; her baby instincts guided her to do so. She felt totally secure when her mother was around, and whatever she did or wherever she played, from the corner of her eye looked out for her all the time. When she could not see her, her voice assured her. And when Miss Mohan held her in a hug, and took God's name, Ranee simply lost all fears. When her mother was there, she could never want anything. Even as she grew, day by day, she felt more and more secure, because her mother was Miss Mohan. Whatever mischief she did, she could get no scolding for she was Miss Mohan's child. The only fear that ever visited

Ranee was 'what would happen if her mother went away', as it normally does in small children; then she would clasp her mother's hand, and gently be rocked to sleep. 'When Mummy is there, nothing can go wrong, no one can harm me or touch me.' And Miss Mohan rocked her, and kissed her and said, "My Ranee is the most precious child in the world; I will never allow anyone to even look at my baby in anger or rebuke."

Soon Ranee was going to play school, a small one run by an Anglo Indian lady, who believed she was actually British. Again, the power of beauty and an officer mother, coupled with her polite nature, made her the darling of all the staff. As she was a quick learner, and had an excellent memory, she was immediately the best student, with whatever little the kindergarten had to teach. She played well too, and fair, and was friendly to all other children.

Ranee loved her mother so much, she never wanted to see her upset because of her. She went the extra bit to make sure Miss Mohan never had to get upset with her. Ever.

Unwanted pregnancies

ANITA WAS not going to get any peace, it seemed. Aman Nursing Home was doing better and better. A whole new wing was added to Meena Madhok's gynaecology wards, a full new floor was being built to house another OT and provide an ICU or Intensive Care Unit for serious and critical cases, especially cardiac and stroke patients. Amit was so proud of his venture. Anita felt very happy for him for he deserved the fruits of his hard work. But she was wary of Dr Meena, who was always busy with loads of cases. Anita observed that she was doing almost six D&Cs (Dilation and Curettage) cases every day. There were many causes for this. It was the most preliminary investigation for a suspected uterine disease, for the lining of the uterus thus procured could be sent for a thorough pathology, which made diagnosis and treatment easier. But also, till then, it was the major method used for conducting an abortion, or MTP, short form for 'Medical Termination of Pregnancy'. Anita felt most cases would be MTPs, so she went through the records which confirmed it.

When Anita spoke to Meena, she was nonchalant. She said, "Ma'am, D&C, we also call our "Dal & Chawal". Without this we cannot cover the expenditure of our extended department. We do help people with unwanted pregnancies, and our rooms show full occupancy. See, people trust us now; we have a reputation too, for people leave cheaper places and come here for better care."

"So good for you, for us," said Anita, and went about her rounds. Something did not fit in. She had now become a healthcare executive, and a good one, but she was still a painter, a creator, who saw things beyond what others could see. She soon discovered what her instincts had warned her about.

Anita was sitting with Meena in her consultaion chamber when Radha came in for a check up. She felt hesitant in Anita's presence, and Anita felt she ought to leave them alone; but curiosity got the better of her, and she said, "I'm Mrs Anita Biswas, the senior administrator here, you can feel comfortable with me." That said, she stayed on.

Radha said, almost in a whisper, "Ma'am, I've missed my period, it is a few days overdue; I want to check if I may be pregnant."

Meena asked her the regular questions—"What was the date of your last menstrual period? Do you have children? How old is your last child? How many boys? How many girls? How long have you been married? Have you had any abortions, natural or induced? What does your husband do? Are you working?" And some more, which a doctor is supposed to ask and get the answers to. It seemed Radha had been married for two years and had a one-year-old daughter. She had now missed her period by just four days. Meena told her to give her urine for testing for pregnancy, and also prescribed some blood tests, and told her to come the next day. All this was very routine, and Anita regretted her suspicions. But three days later, she saw Radha being taken to the OT and upon asking the nurse she was told there was to be a D&C. She unobtrusively strolled in when the anaesthetic came in, and wishing her breezily, she began to scrub, and waited for Meena.

As soon as Meena came, she checked the patient's Blood Pressure, checked her chest with the stethoscope, and confirmed if she was 'nil-by-mouth'(fasting), then nodded to the Anaesthetic, saying, "Ok." The Anaesthetic gave the patient an intravenous injection, before the completion of which the patient had been anaesthetised, which she checked by calling out to her and by checking the pupils of her eyes. After she was asleep, they tied her legs in the stirrups, and simply fitted a couple of sanitary napkins, the nurse tying them firmly. Then Meena gave her an intra muscular injection, and they both left the OT, Meena saying, "She'll start bleeding by the evening or tomorrow morning; you can discharge her by late afternoon, before the evening OPD. She'll be so happy to have had such a painless abortion." They both chuckled.

Anita waited till next morning to talk to the Anaesthetic, who opened up at once; in fact, she expected Anita would be knowing it all along. It seemed there were several ladies who came in, fearing that they were pregnant, and that fear was always apparent. Also, if they already had one or two daughters, the fear was greater, and the doctor could easily guess when the lady was eager to abort the baby. Sometimes, they were really not pregnant, and the period had been delayed due to stress or being undernourished or some other reason, which could be corrected by a simple intra muscular injection, the one that Meena administered to Radha. But they played along with the lady's fear and even when her urine report did not show a pregnancy, they typed a positive report. Seeing that, the lady would often break down, or show her desire not to go ahead with the 'pregnancy'. Then Meena would nonchalantly say that if she wanted an easy and painless abortion, she should have it done as soon as possible, for delay made it riskier. Also the 'pertinent' questions asked by her at the first consultation made the patient's financial position obvious. So, the MTP was done the way Anita had observed, with the patient gaining nothing, except the treatment that was a simple intra muscular injection, and the hospital richer by at least ten to fifteen thousand rupees, depending on which category of room or ward she chose.

This knowledge made Anita feel sick, and when she went to talk to Amit, he said, "What is there to worry in this case? We do not harm the patient in any way; in fact, we free them from the fear of an unwanted pregnancy. These ladies are as responsible for what they get, as we may be. If they used preventive measures, they would not need us; and if they want to keep such things secret from their husbands and families, then they pay for it. Please don't torture your conscience with the problems of the whole world. You'll be surprised at the volume of business unwanted pregnancies create for the medical fraternity all around the world. Unmarried girls, raped girls, adulterous women, careless married women—all keep getting pregnant when they absolutely don't want to. Some have access to help and they can afford a safe MTP, but some come in too late, but then even we don't risk an abortion for them, and say 'sorry'. We get so many cases from the villages and small towns, especially young unmarried girls, sadly so many cases of incest even, where the poor girl does not even know what she has landed into. Then we can also offer to arrange an adoption for their babies, in case they go through the pregnancy and deliver the baby with us. There are also innumerable childless couples who crave the joy of having a baby."

" But isn't there a governmental adoption agency that takes care of adoption formalities? I think you have to go through them if you are to adopt a child," Anita said . Amit replied, "It is very much there, but the process is too tedious and takes ages to go through. We offer a simple solution. When we come across a lady who is ready to give her baby for adoption, and have her delivery done here, we match her with the list of childless couples who want a baby, and shortlist one or two, who we feel would be interested, some demography and looks should match; you know a dark complexioned couple would not look good with a very fair baby, it would obviously not look like their own. Once the delivery is done, we call in the couple who are interested, and if they like to take that baby, we simply make the hospital file in the name of the adopting mother. The natural mother is discharged, and a week later the birth certificate of the baby arrives from the municipal department, naming the foster parents as the natural ones; and who can question that. Complete secrecy is observed. Neither the delivering lady nor the adopting lady ever get to know each other, and they can go home and tell whatever stories they want to their relatives, whatever makes them credible. We are paid a neat fifty thousand bucks by the natural mother, plus hospital charges, and anything from fifty thousand to one lakh from the grateful foster parents. It's cool."

"What if something goes wrong, if someone catches you? What if the baby is not perfectly healthy, or has a congenital disease?"

"That's their luck then. Things can go wrong when it's your own baby too. Besides, the people concerned are usually more secretive than us, so nobody ever comes to know; and think of the hundreds of happy couples who get the happiness of having a baby. Even in Europe, so many doctors help women like this. There were so many unwanted pregnancies during the war, when troops were deployed all over France, Germany, England, everywhere. There abortions are not done for the church does not allow it. So these women were helped to hide their bulging tummies by the churches and hospitals, and the babies given for adoption, with a false name on the birth certificates. Society learns to solve its own problems. Come, I have a very pleasant surprise for you. This time you and Rattna are coming with me to Germany. We will also be taking a holiday in Switzerland. How do you feel now? But this is after we officially open our new second floor block, the ICU, and new OT. I'm planning a 'Havan' followed by the ribbon cutting by the Home Minister. I have been applying some pull to get him to agree."

"That won't be difficult, the old man will be eyeing one of our beds in the ICU for free; he's always falling sick." Anita too got caught up in the happy ceremony to take place, and was duly enticed by the Swiss trip. Though she wondered who was sponsoring it this time. Amit must have read her mind, for he said, "Both Meena and I have drawn some money from the profits for a well deserved holiday after five years of hard work." Anita hugged him; he was such a darling after all.

At the lavish party thrown by them in the evening after the opening, which was attended by some of the biggest names in the medical fraternity, Anita tried Scotch for the first time, and she loved it. She felt she was floating in the air, she felt so light, so pleasant, and happy. That night Rattna was pleased, for her mother slept a peaceful, sound sleep. She even snored though she did smell strange. Rattna thanked God. Next morning, she found Anita at her easel, and she was at it all day, it being a Sunday. Then the next

Saturday, she again indulged in a drink, with similar effect. Soon it became a weekly habit, and one Sunday, Amit took Rattna shopping for new bedroom furniture; she would be sleeping in a separate room now. She sulked for she wanted to be with her mother, but Amit said, "Young ladies like you ought to have your own room, you know, where you can keep your lovely dresses in your own wardrobe, your toys and your Teddies as you like, and you shall have a nice study table to read and write like a proper Miss. And when we go to Switzerland for the holiday, you shall pack your own bag, and bring back gifts of your own choice, and decorate your room." Rattna brightened up. But she realised that the main reason she was being shifted out was to do with her mother's Saturday evening binges.

The trip to Germany was focused on a special training for Amit for learning some new surgical techniques, that were proving to be very successful across Europe. People with acute Arthritis, particularly Rheumatoid arthritis were getting Knee Replacement Surgery done to get permanent relief from pain. Considering the vast prevalence of arthritic knee disease in India, Amit saw a great potential if this sort of surgery could be made available to the population here. Again, the partner company in Germany were also manufacturers of the implants needed, so this special arrangement for him to learn the new technique was made for him, and doctors from Germany would assist him from time to time. It would be a pioneering stride for his career, and Amit was hopeful of earning both name and fame, if the procedure would be successful. It was to be a total win-win situation.

The Swiss holiday was a delight; only the really lucky Indians could afford it too. The whole country looked like a series of picture postcards. The green of the valleys was like no other green in the world; the flowers were in such intense colours that Anita wanted to start painting them right away; the lakes were the blue colour of the sky, and the hills took one's breath away. Each day had something more awesome in store. The Scotch and wine flowed freely. It was the greatest week ever for Amit and Anita, and Rattna was on top of the world, framing in her mind the sentences she would utter to impress her friends while recounting her experiences.

Back home, Amit got busy making up for the lost time at the hospital, and it being Meena's turn to go on a holiday, working with her substitute kept him very busy. Busy enough not to realise that Anita was drinking almost every day. It was important that the work at the hospital did not lag, and Anita was good at that.Only Rattna noticed that though her mother seemed to look relaxed, she actually looked weak; drink was really draining her, not empowering her. But she did sleep well, and that might do some good. Poor child, she was left pondering on the cruelties of life.

In a corner of her mind, a possibility began to be created: Rattna would not like to be either a doctor, or an artist.

The claim

RANEE MUST have been about six when her whole world was shaken by one cruel sentence. She was eating her lunch, while the cook and her Ayah chatted in the kitchen. She was about to call out for some water when she heard the cook say, "Ranee baby is so sweet, so fair and beautiful, and madam is just the opposite—how can they be mother and daughter?"

And the Ayah said, "She is adopted, she is not her real daughter." And Ranee almost choked. She realised that Miss Mohan never answered her question when she asked for her father.

She would say, "He is very far away but you will meet him; I will take you there." She could not believe what she had heard in the kitchen. These people were mean. Just because her mother was not beautiful, they were saying mean things. She would tell Mamma, and then they would be taught a lesson. In the night when they were settling into their mosquito net, she told her mother what she had heard, and Mamma said, "Say your prayers and go to sleep, my love, we will talk tomorrow."

The next day, they sat in the tiny veranda and Miss Mohan told her, "You know I never tell lies; you are my very own daughter, whom I love the most in the world, but it is true that you were not born to me, I have adopted you."

"But why?" asked Ranee, not comprehending this new thing in her life.

"Because I love you, and I wanted a baby of my own to love, to bring up, to be my companion." And hugging her, she gave her comfort. But the demon had entered into Ranee's life, forever.

Some time after this, events turned again in Miss Mohan's life. At the time of the partition of India into India and Pakistan, people chose which country they would live in, but the terrible riots left them with only one concern, the safety of their lives, and they migrated en masse leaving behind their belongings, their land and holdings, their bank balances and lockers—the only concern was to avoid being killed, and reach the 'other side' safely. Over the following years, the governments of both countries exchanged records about the properties and other accounts, and began to reimburse the people who had thus crossed over, with land and money of more or less the same value that they had left behind. Very painstakingly and patiently, both governments tallied the records with each other, decided how they would reimburse these people, acquired land with government finance, or took over the land left behind by those who had migrated to the other country, then, even more painstakingly traced the people who had taken refuge wherever they could, and were dispatching registered letters to them to come and claim their rights. Miss Mohan had also been traced, and being Satnam's widow and successor, had been allotted his share of their village land, and had received her "Claim" in a registered letter. It brought tears to her eyes, and she sat motionless for hours, pondering over the past. There is never any adversity, she thought—the whole of nature connives to move us towards our destiny.

After much deliberation, she decided she would go and accept her 'claim', as these disbursements were called. It was Satnam's right and she deserved it; besides, she had a lovely child who deserved to inherit her property. She duly arranged for train bookings, asked for leave at her office and Ranee's school, sent a telegram informing Kartar, and also requesting him to accompany her to Patiala, near which city she was to be given some agricultural land. Ranee was very excited to be travelling, but could not stop grappling with the new word that had entered her life—'adopted'. Why was she adopted? How could she be adopted? Why would anyone take someone else's child? Why would anyone give away their child? She did not believe it at all. Maybe her real mother had died, she imagined in her tiny mind, and this made sense to her, for there was a boy in her class at school who had said that his mother was dead and his grandmother took care of him. She was sure it must have been so. Or maybe her mother was too poor, like the small boy who came to beg for food every afternoon outside her school. But his mother still kept him with her, she did not give him away. Maybe her mother was even poorer. And Mamma did love her the most, so she must have 'adopted' her. Mamma was the only real mother she knew—she was the best, and got the best things for Ranee, and everyone was kind to her because they were told to be so by Mamma. But Mamma never took anything from anyone, so she could not have just taken Ranee from her real mother. There were a hundred explanations for all her probabilities, but there was no explanation for the fact that she was adopted.

There was so much preparation for the journey. Mamma did so much shopping, buying gifts for her friend in Amritsar, and for her children, buying new dresses for Ranee, collecting food items that would stay fresh during the long journey, packing bedrolls for sleeping on the train berths—she felt like it was a festival. They left with two of their domestic helps, the Ayah who travelled with them in the first class and took care of Ranee's every whim, and Raju who travelled second class, but rushed to them at every station, and helped with the luggage and the bedrolls. After a fascinating journey, they reached Amritsar, and Kartar was there to receive them at the station. He took them home in his big car, which he drove, and his chauffeur drove the second car with the helps and the luggage. Ranee was anyway used to such luxury. Reaching home, Miss Mohan rushed in to meet Anjana, and they both hugged each other and wept. Then she called all Anjana's children and hugged them except the big boys, who touched her feet and took her blessings. When Anjana took Ranee in her embrace, her eyes moist, Ranee felt the warmth of her bosom. She kept looking into Anjana's eyes, and running her little hand over her forehead and face; she hugged her tight. The vibrations she got seemed to answer many questions, but they seemed to ask many more questions. Later in the night when they sat around chatting after dinner, she again sat in Anjana's lap, putting her head on her shoulder, and whispered in her ear, "Are you my mother?" Anjana only wept; she would not reply. But Ranee just knew. And she wondered.

Next day, Miss Mohan left with Kartar for Patiala, and located the village they had to reach. They looked for the

'Patwari', the man who is entrusted with the land records by the government. He was already expecting them, for Kartar had sent him a telegram. The Patwari showed Miss Mohan the papers of her land deed. Kartar verified that she was indeed Mohini who had changed her name when escaping from Pakistan, and then he took them to see the actual land. There was a tract of some sixty acres of land, out of which she was getting twenty, the other forty having been given to Satnam's two brothers. He pointed them out as they were already working on their part of the land. Noticing her, they came towards her, and with folded hands greeted her; she was overcome with loathing and contempt for them, remembering that horrible night. Her eyes clouded, but she overcame her feelings, and though she did return the greeting, her eyes burnt with controlled anger as she straightened herself and held her head high. She was way too powerful for them now.

Word of her coming had spread, and two young men came with their wives and children to meet her, and touching her feet, said, "How are you Didi, you have not recognized us, we are your own brothers." And she marvelled how handsome and dapper they had turned out to be. They took them all home, and tearfully told her how their parents had refused to leave the village come what may, as their daughter had mysteriously disappeared, and they wanted to be home if she ever came back. When the rioters had come seeking Hindu blood, the two young boys had hidden inside two huge 'Tandoors', which had been specially installed for Mohini's wedding, to make scores of tandoori rotis for the guests, and were since lying unused. The parents could not hide and were hounded out of the house and killed. She looked at Kartar who nodded, and she knew that he had known all along, but she had never asked, and he had never told her. She sighed and quietly mourned her parents, and realised she could be responsible for their cruel death. She thanked God for saving her brothers. They spent the night with her brothers, and left next morning, appointing them legally to till her land on her behalf, and promising to visit them again soon.

That night, Ranee did not sleep. She knew she had found her real mother, but could not reconcile the facts. She was not poor, she was not sick, and she was not dead either; then why had she given her away? Obviously, Mamma had not robbed her from her mother, so, even that did not make sense; Mamma never took anything from anyone. And Anjana was so happy with Mamma. She would have hated Mamma if she had taken away Ranee forcibly. Did she not like her when she was born? That could not be for she had five more children, one even younger to her, and she loved them all. Besides, Ranee was the prettiest child, so how could she not like her? Her mind argued the possible reasons why she was given away, and decided maybe Anjana was just too selfish, and did not bother about bringing her up, for she remembered Mamma saying that she had wanted to bring up Ranee and had wanted her to be her child. That was it; Anjana did not want Ranee, and Miss Mohan wanted her. Mamma loved her so much, cared for her so much, she was the perfect mother, and Ranee loved her. But the heart wrenching feeling of rejection as a small baby, formed a lump in her tiny chest and stayed with her.

Her judgement was made condemning Anjana, and condoning Mamma. Done quite simply in her mind. She had stopped being terrified of the word 'adopted'. She would never forgive Anjana for giving her away, and she would always love Mamma for 'adopting' her.

Whatever psychologists and psychiatrists may say, a person's character is developed in the first eight or ten years of his life. Experiences and perceptions gained in the first three years transcend words and language, action and reaction, conflict and dilemma; the growing brain devours all the knowledge passing around, in sounds, in visions, reflexes, vibrations, positive and negative currents, created by the people and creatures around, the objects around—all elements of nature.When a ten-month-old baby throws a tantrum, he's learnt it right here; when a three-year-old tells a lie, he's learnt it all here; every moment their brains are growing, learning, filtering information, memorising, and their behavioural 'survival kits' are being created. The devils and angels are all there, working on the growing child and taking their places in his mind. He is grasping it all, and imbibing it into the sub-conscious mind, permanently. A prancing baby rabbit sniffs danger and runs into the foliage for safety, he's learnt it all here, from all the elements of nature. Sometimes our eyes are shut, but if someone stares at us, we just come to know; do we wonder how? Do we believe the growing baby is dumb until he or she begins to speak? Though he cannot communicate, his mind knows what's going on, and he can make his judgements too. The baby observes behaviour, and his own behaviour patterns are getting created, very subtly, but surely. Like Ranee made hers, and they went on to be a part of her character.

Miss Mohan arrived back the next day, and a day later they left for Dhanbad, for Miss Mohan had innumerable responsibilities for the miners there and she was a really busy lady. She was happy after this trip; the meeting with Satnam's brothers had been cathartic for her, and meeting her own brothers was the best thing to have happened. She now had ownership of a huge piece of land, had discovered her lost family, met her friend—what more could she ask for?

Ranee, meanwhile, was coming to terms with the fact that she had been forsaken by her real mother, and her resentment only grew. Rushing through school, homework and play, it never left her; it had an impact on all her thinking; and her thoughts got darker day by day. She began to be suspicious instead of trusting, curious instead of believing, not sure whether people were true or pretending. All she could be sure of was her Mamma, and though she remembered the soft and warm touch of Anjana's embrace, she was happy in the strength and security of Mamma's arms. She began to grow really fast now, getting taller and prettier. She could perceive the power Miss Mohan had in society, at home, with colleagues, even high ranking officers and ministers, and she learnt how to use the reflected power it gave her.

She began to think of herself as a grown up lady, and imagined the sort of person she was going to be. She knew she was going to be very pretty, and intelligent, but she was going to be efficient and powerful like Mamma. She would be hard working and excel in everything, and whatever else she did , she would never do anything to annoy Mamma, she would always be in her good books. Even try to make her proud of her. She behaved very well at home and at school got excellent grades, but gradually turned into a frightful bully for other children. She hated the children who were living with their own parents; she was jealous of them. Subconsciously, she was filled with venom which overflowed in vicious ways. She would twist some child's arm for no reason, and then walk away; pinch someone till the child's tears appeared, and again walk away. For her teachers and other grown-ups, she was the epitome of good behaviour, but with children she began to be a terror. The same kids whom she had loved before, now simply towed her line. They all wondered what had changed her. They believed she was so arrogant because her mother ranked so high in society.

As she reached the age of ten, strange curiosities began to rise in her mind; she was curious about all parts of her own body, and wondered what other children looked like under their clothes. In fact, one day, she actually bullied the Ayah's son into removing his clothes. She thought she could hurt him harder, but she felt disgusted and ashamed of herself after that; thankfully, he never came to their house again, and Ayah told her that he had been sent to the Military School by Miss Mohan.

The same year, she was sent to the hostel in Darjeeling. Mamma had sat and spoken to her, "A girl needs to go to a good High School to get good grooming, like your Mamma did. We do not have great schools in Dhanbad, and I cannot leave my job, but you need to go to a good convent, to learn

English language well, and good manners and behaviour—sports too, for which I have decided to send you to this lovely school in Darjeeling. The climate there is wonderful. There are lovely hills and valleys, colourful flowers, and the school on the hillside is beautiful. You will love to hear the wind whistling through the trees, and the birds twitter outside your window every morning. Also, I will come to meet you every month, so we will not miss each other much. Darling, I have no one except you, even I cannot live without you, but I have to prepare you for a bright future—maybe you can become a doctor like me, and maybe I can send you to London to do a speciality degree course. For all this you basically need a good school." As a whole month went by preparing for the hostel, shopping for all that the school asked for in a long list, the whole household--Mamma, Ranee and the staff, all were super excited. When she left with Mamma to join the new school, to be away from her for most of the next six years, Ranee had mixed feelings, a little insecurity, but a sense of liberty, a feeling of being grown up enough to be sent away to study.

Darjeeling is the most beautiful place on earth, she felt, and all the girls in the convent were pretty and wealthy; Ranee really belonged there. So much activity happened all the time; the years just flew, so that at the end of school, Ranee had shaped into a confident young lady, beautiful and tall, well educated, poised, intelligent and exceptionally well groomed; also presumptious, pompous, lonely, nasty and quite a bully. Meanwhile, Miss Mohan had risen in her career to become the Inspector of Mines, an authority almost as high as the governor of the state, for she governed all the mines of the region, and mines made for the largest part of the commerce there. She was faithful to her responsibilities, and saw to it that the work conditions in the mines improved, and also played a major role in forming of co-operatives, allowing both the owners and workers to earn better. All mine owners, big and small were in awe of her, and also afraid of her; one negative report from her could simply have their mines shut down, and she had too much integrity and honesty to be compromised by anyone. Meanwhile, Ranee had decided to learn medicine for she wanted to be as powerful as Mamma, and was genuinely curious about the human body. So, after a month at home, she left for the next hostel in a medical college in the largest city of India.

Ranee joins Amit

AMIT'S HOSPITAL was getting more and more profitable; he now had two chemist shops within the premises, and the profit on the sale of medicines prescribed in the hospital felt like loot; he wondered why he had not thought of it before. He realized that now he was not a doctor meant to heal people, but was more a businessman, meant to create profits. He was proud of his hospital, it was one of the best in the city, though private players were still very few. People still looked to the government to provide healthcare. A new era was dawning in medical history; what was in the realm of fiction and fantasy had become a reality. Organ transplants were happening successfully across Europe, and Dr Christian Barnard had successfully done a heart transplant as well. Though heart transplant surgery could be said to be still in the embryonic stage, kidney transplants were doing well. He had been approached by one Dr Agarwal, to set up a kidney transplant unit in Aman Nursing Home, and Amit was excited. He could see tremendous potential in the new surgery, the number of nephrology patients was rising, and he could see people lining up for surgeries. He could also see the earnings from one transplant being equal to a hundred bone surgeries. But his partners in Germany had turned down the proposal. They were afraid that in a country like India, where laws were lax and implemented even less, there would be a possibility of organ trade happening, which could lead to enquiries and expose their connection with Amit.

Amit was peeved now with their constant interference in his work. He was slogging to make the hospital do better and better, and knew his business well. There were also those Germans who would always be occupying one or two of the corner rooms, and they were never patients. He had to be sure no other doctor went into their room, and only the most trustworthy nurses went in to give them medicines which they never swallowed; they were duly flushed down the toilets. He had to make fake case files for all of them, cooking up fictitious diseases and fictitious treatments, fictitious pathology reports and all on fictitious names; he never ever knew the real name of any of these 'guests'. But it had been an unwritten part of the contract with the German company and he had to play along. He was told they were in India to do business; that they were businessmen, but he always wondered. And he also wondered if some day they could get him into trouble. But he had to credit the Germans for their help in setting up the hospital and the successive expansions. The ICU had shown tremendous potential in treating people and in making money. The doctors were prescribing thrice the amount of medicines for each patient than they actually needed, and while his own shops sold them and he made money, the unused medicines came back on the shelf, and he again made money.

He argued with the Germans that if he did not start transplants at Aman, the hospital would lose out on other business also. He had added Cat-Scan equipment and Dialysis equipment, and technicians for them too, so it would be tough to pay for their upkeep if they did not do the relevant surgeries, and also competition would leave them behind.

After a trip to Germany, specially made to convince them, they did agree to let him start transplants, but strictly forbade any organ trade; he had to commit that only operations with genuine donors like blood relatives would be done. Amit didn't mind; he was relieved they had relented. Besides, he would be able to maintain a clean image in the healthcare market. 'It's ok, you give some, you gain some,' he thought, but he had gained a lot and was comfortable with the arrangement.

It was late afternoon on a Saturday, and he was sitting alone, making mental plans for the new transplant ward, the space, the equipment, the medical and technical staff needed for it, and the best specialist surgeons he would have to attract to his venture.

"May I come in?" said a smart young lady, and walked into his room without waiting for a reply. She halted before taking a seat, and he gestured that she may sit.

"I am Miss Ranee Mohan, final year student at the Central Medical Institute and Research Centre. How do you do, Dr Biswas?" Amit was looking her over—she was so pretty and confident. Looking at her a thought passed his mind that some years from now, his Rattna could be looking just like this. She would also be on the threshold of life. And he suddenly missed his daughter.

He craved to be able to spend more time with her, and made a mental note that he would. And then he thought of Anita—she too was neglected, and she needed him so much. She had always simply leaned on him, never asserted or imposed herself, always accepted his decisions. She was looking more and more tired now, and less and less cheerful, except when there was a glass of scotch by her side.

Maybe he should never have got her involved in the hospital business, it was too much hard work, though she was doing it competently, but the strain was showing a lot.

She would have been perfect as a simple housewife, bringing up Rattna, socialising a little, and painting for a hobby—a relaxed life was what she was built for. And suddenly he realised this young lady was waiting, and she had quietly waited for him to come back from his mental sojourn, the pleasant smile still on her face.

'Good grooming,' thought Amit. "Sorry, and what can I do for you?"

"My college will be accepting placements from different hospitals for the internship of us final year students, and I want you to select me to do my internship at your hospital. I have decided that I would like to work at your nursing home. That's all."

"And what makes you believe that I will do as you say?" Amit could not conceal the surprise in his voice.

"Because I have studied the working of your hospital; it does much better business than other hospitals. You have a dynamic team, but you could do much better with some aggressive marketing and dedicated administration. I have an interest in both these fields, and not much interest in patient caring and curing. I would create a department for Hospitality Management in your hospital, and with my marketing skills, double your business in no time."

When she said 'administration', Amit actually felt tempted, for it could achieve some relief for Anita, she was so overworked; and he was surprised at what the girl had said; it made sense, but an intern is supposed to learn the business of being a good doctor, a healer, not an administrator.

"I shall see what I can do. I will remember your offer, and discuss it with my team, and thanks for coming."

But the meeting was being conducted by Ranee, and she said, "I know you will not discuss it with Mrs Biswas, and Dr Madhok will jump at my proposal when I tell her the details. The people at my college will appoint me as I direct them to, and you will also make up your mind soon, so see you later." And then she took her leave, leaving Amit wondering if he was weak, or the young lady was too headstrong.

That evening he actually went home early, and spent hours talking to Rattna, walked with her and even played with her, and loved doing just that. He wished he could spend time with his daughter more often, and decided to do it now, for time was flying away, and with it her sweet simple childhood. Once she grew up, he would be left searching for his little baby. That night, when he put his arm round Anita's shoulders, he realised she was putting on a lot of weight, and that was not good at all.

Predictably, Ranee joined Aman Nursing Home as a Junior Intern and announced to Amit that she had no intention of working towards a post graduation. She had decided to work with him exactly as she had said, in administration and marketing. The first year she spent making herself very useful to Anita, and quickly learning all there was to the working of the hospital. She gradually gained the loyalty of most of the staff, and Meena Madhok's affection too. She did not fit in like any intern—she automatically fitted in with the managerial and organisational specialists, and began to show improvement in the running of the place. No one was now inclined to be seen wasting time, her discipline rubbed off on everyone, and Anita passed on more and more responsibilities and important decisions to her, taking things easy after a long time. The year passed, and now that she was Dr Ranee Mohan, her respect with everyone grew.

"Now I should start the real work," she said to Amit, "we have to double our clientele fast."

"What do you propose?" said Amit.

"I propose to travel abroad and get us patients from across the world. There are hundreds of people waiting their turn for surgeries like knee transplant, kidney transplant, hysterectomies, whatever does not come under emergency surgery, in England alone. They are covered by the Medical Insurance, so their treatment is free, but they have to wait for their turn, which goes on for several months. Most of these people are in their fifties and sixties, which means they are financially still productive, and their disease is stalling their financial future too. We can do their surgeries for a fraction of what it would cost them if they had to get it done privately in their own country—they just need to be cajoled to travel to India, get operated, get cured and fly back for some few thousand pounds, and be back at work. Simple."

"And how does this 'simple' cajoling happen?"

"Again, simple. There are hundreds of Indian doctors working at all hospitals there. They can be 'induced' to make a suggestion to the prospective patients, and later convince the ones who show interest. Allow me to make a few trips, and I will show you the results. All the oil rich people from the Middle East go to England and the USA and pay truckloads of money for their treatments and their stay there. They can all be persuaded to come here instead, and one satisfied batch will spread the word and then you will never have enough capacity. And, of course, we have to give the hospital smart interiors, and improve the hygiene too, so that we can go in for quicker discharges. There's lots more logistics to work out, once our mind is made up. Well, my mind is made up, I'm waiting for you to affirm."

Amit called a meeting of all his attending and visiting surgeons, and Ranee quickly convinced them all, and the vision of the lucre flying in got all of them to agree; it was time now for another quantum growth. Meanwhile, Anita getting fonder and fonder of Ranee invited her to live in their house as they had a spare room next to their own. Ranee was so polite and well behaved, she was a delight to have around.

When Miss Mohan heard of this, she came over to visit her daughter. She lived at the accommodation the government provided her with, and agreed to visit the Biswas family for dinner. The visit to the hospital in the day had surprised her; she could see a lot of medical activity and polite disciplined staff, spruced up shelves at the nursing stations, everything almost perfect. Ranee proudly showed her around, and as they passed the Operation theatres, Ranee mentioned to her mother that the famous Dr Rao, a pulmonary surgeon, was operating on a woman that day, for a patch of cancer on her right lung. Miss Mohan had not seen any women lung cancer patients, but she thought it was likely to be tied to an urban lifestyle, like women smoking too much, or some other reason. But there was smoking in smaller towns and villages too, so many women were addicted to 'beedis'. She guessed they probably never got diagnosed or simply puffed away to their graves.

"Can I see him perform the operation?" she asked Ranee, "It invokes an academic interest in me."

"Sure," said Ranee, and organised a scrub for her to stand as an observer in the OT. Miss Mohan watched the eminent surgeon go through the whole surgery with amazing precision and swift motions, ensuring little blood loss, and going through to the last suture with equal diligence, as he looked at the time and waved to the anaesthetic, while pulling off his mask and preparing to leave.

She introduced herself and congratulated him on his proficiency as a surgeon, but in her mind she wondered why he had chosen to complete the sutures himself, when the assisting surgeon is supposed to do it. Besides, she noticed that the assisting surgeon had not moved at all during the operation. He had simply stood rooted to his spot, and she wondered. Some time later, she saw him in the drive, putting Dr Rao's medical bag, and other equipment in the car, and said, "You are Dr Rao's assistant, right?"

He said, "I am Dr Rao's chauffeur, Madam, Dr Sahib does not use an assistant."

"But you were in the OT as the assistant; I saw you,"she persisted.

He told her, "Dr Sahib gets twenty thousand rupees for an operation, and ten thousand for the assistant; so I stand in, and he gets to keep both the fees, and I get a tiny tip too."

He seemed to see nothing wrong in it, but Miss Mohan was appalled. How could they tolerate such gross negligence, such a blatant disregard of rules, such a huge risk for the patient. She thought she would point it out to Ranee, or Amit, but paused, for she realized that they already knew. The nagging feeling that something was not right, began to take a hazy shape.

They sat relaxed in Amit's beautiful sitting room, and Miss Mohan spoke of her concern. "I have made this trip for a specific reason; I cannot accept that Ranee has not registered for the post graduate programme, in this day and age when people are requiring super specialists—what can be the future for a mere MBBS? Ranee has to still give me a valid reason to convince me. Though you are an adult now, my child, I still wish to be a part of your future plans and wish that you should pursue greater heights in your career."

Amit wondered what Ranee would tell her mother, and Ranee said, " Mamma, I can never lie to you, nobody can. I have not registered as I really did not wish to study any more. I cannot force myself to do so much hard work, at least not yet. I have worked very hard up till now; I wish to relax for some time, and maybe find some other calling in life."

"And have you found the other calling?" asked her mother.

Ranee said, "I am thinking of many things; something will turn up. I am working in a hospital, gaining experience and being productively occupied. Meanwhile, I am with this wonderful family. They have even taken me into their home and look after me very well."

Miss Mohan looked around at them all—the sadly feeble Anita, so much goodness in her, good moral and social values, but a weak back, unable to make strong decisions, or stand by any; exhausting herself at such a young age from work she never wanted to do, not doing what she actually wanted to do, and now obviously leaning upon liquor to find some solace; very sad. She could have been a happier and contented lady, a proud mother and wife, again very sad. She felt the most wonderful person in the family was Rattna. The girl was well grounded, well behaved, confident and quite in charge of herself. She obviously knew her mind, could make important decisions and abide by them too, and remarkably, felt responsible for her mother; almost subconsciously, her eyes never left her mother, she was so concerned for her. This child drew more respect than anyone else.

And Rattna was awfully impressed by Miss Mohan, her strong silent personality—her impressive crisp sari, and the leather bag and smart shoes, complementing her style statement. She looked as important as she was, and was obviously much more powerful than she seemed to be; this was the person Rattna wished to be when she grew up. The young girl made the most important decision of her life, and committed herself to stick by her decision, come what may. A strange bond seemed to be forming between these two—the young Rattna and the sensitive Miss Mohan, who observed the changing contours of the girl's face as new thoughts came and went. A new ambition was being created in her mind and determination had set in.

'This child has immense potential,' she thought and invited her to come and sit close to her, and gave her an encouraging hug. She knew when to assert herself, and when to let go. So she decided to travel back to Dhanbad the next day, giving Ranee time to introspect and choose her track in life. Just before leaving, she told Ranee, "There is talk of shifting me, as a special advisor to the Central Health Ministry. The huge advance in medical treatments, the flourishing private sector, hundreds of new private hospitals and nursing homes, have created a need for the government to form new laws and norms to guard against malpractices by medical and paramedical professionals;

even the big pharmaceutical industry needs to be governed by new guidelines. Basically, the government needs to keep up with the strides made by the advanced medical fraternity, but being shackled by ancient laws, they have no teeth, so a group of us experienced doctors are being designated to advise and guide the Ministry. I shall tell you when the official order comes. Being in Delhi, I will feel more easily approachable than being in Dhanbad, and you are all I have in this world; otherwise, for me it makes no difference where I work. Bye for now, and may God help you always."

To Anita she said, "You are like my daughter, and I bless you and will always pray for you." To Amit she said, "You have a wonderful wife, take good care of her; she is the pillar of your home, and of your career. God bless you both."

International growth

TWO SEPARATE flights were booked by the staff of Aman Nursing Home—one for Ranee to travel to the Middle East countries and London, and the other for Dr Meena Madhok and an associate to travel to the USA and then to UK to learn the latest technique of making test-tube babies, or IVF, short for In-Vitro-Fertilisation—the new treatment that was helping people who had lost all hope, to finally have a chance to have a baby of their own.

People had got over the awe and disbelief of 'test-tube babies', and IVF was a household word now. Even middle class people had begun to aspire for the benefits of IVF aided babies. Women well past their prime, couples who had shut all doors on hopes of having a child, were again hopeful, and the new technology was giving good results. Though not every couple who tried was blessed, but enough people were benefitting to keep hopes high and people queueing up at IVF centres. India also had the advantage of lax litigation about the procedure, and culturally the craze of having a child at any cost, like folks selling their land and gold to pay for the costly IVF treatment, promised a healthy market to Amit, making it a hugely lucrative job for the doctors. The stresses of urbanisation, land, water and air pollution reducing fertility among the population was taking the graph of the industry thus born higher and higher. Not to be left behind, Dr Meena made the special trip abroad to train in the latest procedures, and start a state-of-the-art IVF Centre at Aman, the construction for which had already begun, with cash flowing in from Germany. She returned in six months and the new facility was opened with due fanfare and celebrity ribbon-cutting the following January. Anita was overawed, and young Rattna realized how popular and famous her father was, and loved him for being such a good dad in spite of being so busy. But the limelight belonged to Meena, for her department now was the biggest showpiece at Aman, for the first time since it's inception.

IVF means a lot more than enabling childless couples to have babies. It has spurned a huge industry by itself, again due to the liberal laws in the country, and with the connivance of a whole lot of people at different strata of society. In the natural process, a woman's ovaries, where all her ova are stored, cause one ovum to mature every month; this matured ovum is then released into the fallopian tube, where it gets fertilized by one of the millions of sperm ejaculated in her vagina, which successfully travels to the tube. This fertilized embryo then comes down to the uterus, where it lodges itself, and grows on to become a baby. When all is not well, this does not happen. A woman may have a healthy ovum being secreted by the ovary, and also have a healthy uterus, but may still not get pregnant if her fallopian tubes are blocked or malformed. Then her ovaries are monitored daily, and when the ovum is at the right level of maturity, it is removed surgically, and fertilized by a healthy sperm, obtained from her husband's semen, in a laboratory, and successfully planted into her healthy uterus; thus making her pregnant, and helping the couple to become happy parents.

The problems arise when sometimes the male does not have adequate sperm, or weak ones or even malformed ones which can never fertilize an ovum, or if they did, would result in a malformed foetus. Or the female may not be producing ova, due to malformed or diseased ovaries, or due to a premature menopause; or her uterus could be unfit for pregnancy due to a range of reasons. It could be a congenital condition of a retroverted uterus, or due to some disease like fibroids and tumours, or even cancer. In such cases, the doctors turn to the 'facilitators' in the industry; if the needy millions could contribute so many kidneys and other organs for transplant to critical patients, would arranging sperm donors, ova donors, even surrogate mothers be difficult? The couple has to have a baby, whatever it takes, whatever it costs. Secrecy is their only mandate. Often their closest relatives will not know. Miraculously, a man will boast of a successor, and a woman proudly say, "God is kind, better late than never." Often a pious and godly sadhu would take the credit for the prayers and blessings that went to obtain this happiness. As they say, 'In science, what can be done, will be done; damn the parameters of morality, sociology, legality, even humanity.' Starting slowly with the word spreading by successful treatments, Meena began to get a regular stream of patients at her IVF centre, and her expertise got better and better.

A satisfied Amit began to concentrate on Ranee. He had to make sure she would justify all the expense of her trips abroad. She had started by visiting Iran, Kuwait, and Dubai. These countries already had a huge Indian population, and she had checked out all acquaintances living there. She charmed them all into introducing her to medical professionals, and it was not difficult to persuade them to induce prospective patients to consider India, specifically

Aman Nursing Home, before travelling west. "Just show them the huge savings, and our pictures and the presentation I will leave with you; add to it our facility of offering accommodation for post-operative and post-procedural care, at very little cost. They won't need much pushing," she told her contacts. She also offered them liberal cash backs and other perks, like a free trip to see the Taj Mahal after every fifty patients sent by them.

A sprinkling of patients began to arrive at Aman's hospital for different treatments and surgeries, few and far between at first, but as these few returned satisfied, his name spread by word of mouth, and more and more people came in. Ranee took care to keep her contacts in good books, and they in turn gave more and more business to Aman; it was going well for everybody—the patients were happy, their local doctors were happy, Ranee was happy and Aman was very happy.

Then Ranee moved on to London. This was going to be tough for she was going to be up against State Healthcare and State Health Insurance. She would have to convince people who would be getting treated free, and with better facilities, to instead pay for their treatment, and that too in an under developed country like India. Here her moves had to be planned differently. Two days after she arrived in London, she contacted Ravi, her friend from medical college. He had been the hearthrob of every girl in college, but he had admired only Ranee, and she had at best been just cordial with him. He was also the best student, and she had never rubbed him the wrong way like she had done with other boys; with them she had been ruthless. She would seduce them to the point of, well, actually having sex, and then give them the snub, leaving them panting for her, drooling for her. She simply enjoyed the power she had over them, snubbing them, seducing them again, pretending to be a sweet young girl who stopped just short of a sexual act, sometimes daring them to try to seduce her. Innumerable games she played with most boys and girls were somehow never played with Ravi.

Even then, she remembered her own trauma. She would imagine herself as a foetus growing in Anjana's belly, imagine herself being born in her house, being suckled at her breast, and then being wrapped in a towel and given away---and a shard of lightning would pass through her mind and body. Singed with pain, she would just sit still, her eyes burning, pouring blood instead of tears. No reasoning, no reassurance, love or comfort could repair the fracture that broke her heart that day, years ago, in Amritsar. And now she led a life of incomplete relationships.

She contacted Ravi who was now a radiologist at a hospital in east London. He was thrilled to hear from her, and they decided to meet the next day. She met him at the coffee shop in India House, to which she had access, being Miss Mohan's daughter, and he was duly impressed. After the pleasantries, she began to spin her well rehearsed yarn.

She told him she was working for the Indian Medical Association, in the capacity of a consultant, and they were doing a research project upon the doctors of Indian origin working across UK and USA Their aim was to find what better facilities they were enjoying abroad, and whether provided the same, they could be persuaded to work in India. The new India, where economic reforms were happening, could be a satisfying destination for these doctors, and also for several patients too.

"Well," said Ravi, "for this you have to simply get the Directory, and pick up the whole list; with your designation, you should have no problem in contacting or interviewing them."

"I think if I was introduced to them by common friends, they would be more forthcoming about their experiences," said Ranee. "You could introduce me to the doctors you know, along with some European doctors too, for the sake of a comparative study, and they could get me to meet some of their acquaintances, and so on. I plan to wrap up my work in two to four weeks; it's costing the IMA a lot to keep me here for so long."

She threw such a pretty cover over her actual purpose. Ravi was ready to throw his soul at her feet, and she had asked for something so minimal, he was overcome.

"Of course I will do all I can," he said, wanting to extend her an invitation to move in with him, albeit to avoid the expense of living at a hotel, but decided to wait, afraid of offending her. Every evening after work, he would introduce her to a few friends. During the day he would be arranging meetings for her, and she would choose whom she could target into helping her to outsource some patients to India, who would be greedy enough or gullible enough to fall for her schemes, and to her charm. Within two weeks, she did manage to get a handful of people interested in coming to India for treatment; some were tired of waiting their turn for surgeries for painful arthritic joints, some did not have adequate insurance, some had nobody to care for them and fell for the lure of cheap nursing care, and Ranee knew she was going to succeed even in London.

Quite euphoric, she accepted Ravi's invitation to spend the weekend with him. They would go on an overnight trip to Paris. "Okay, I'll come with you, but with a promise that we will not talk about work at all," she told him. She had to be very sure she never dropped her guard, or let slip the real purpose of her visit. They spent the day sightseeing, strolling past the several art galleries, visited the Louvre, enjoyed coffee and the exotic French pastries at the café filled with chattering Frenchmen, then reverted to their hotel rooms to rest before dinner. Ravi took her for dinner to a cozy French restaurant, where the music was soft, the decor Victorian, and the cutlery sterling silver; the perfect romantic outing. Over the evening, she never realized how she slowly succumbed to the influence of the exotic champagne they were served, warming up with foie-gras and succulent cheese; and Ravi's soft conversation and cute jokes that made her chuckle. He lovingly held her elbow and chaperoned her to her room, where he sat on the couch while she changed.

They kissed softly, and then passionately, and Ravi said, "You made me wait all those years for this, I've been craving for you forever." And Ranee sighed in agreement, and held him closer. He began to rub her shoulders and she gave herself up to all his sensuous manoeuvres. He rubbed her back, kneading her flesh with his palm, while he slowly undressed her. He massaged her buttocks, and ran his hands down the back of her legs, kissed her toes, sucking on them one by one, while she felt quite helpless with the erotic treat, and a newly found romance. Turning her over, he tickled her belly, kissed her breasts and rubbed her thighs, till she was ignited with passion, and then she experienced her first full act of sex, orgasm and all, till panting they both flopped together on the fragrant silk sheets, while the lights illuminated the Eiffel Tower outside their window. Before he passed out, Ravi said, "Why did all the college boys say you were frigid?"

And she said, "A case of sour grapes perhaps."

She sat on the couch, thinking, and wondering why she had kept herself from the ultimate pleasure of a sexual experience till now, and suddenly realized the kind of power she could exercise over people, in the throes of passion. She had a new weapon in her inventory now, and people who could not be cajoled with cash, she would learn to seduce otherwise.

Back in London, she decided to wind up as much work as she could in a week, for she had a budget to fit, and the first batch of patients were ready to file papers to travel to India. They were happy; Aman was happy; the contacts in London were happy at the kickbacks, and Aman would never know how much kept pouring into her pockets with every venture.

Anita's alcoholism

AMAN SPENT his Sunday morning day-dreaming about the new set of patients that would come in from England now; how many times higher he would charge them, how much money he would make on the accommodation he would arrange for them to live in for post-operative care, and how many more doctors he would attach to his hospital. He even began to think of the next expansion. Rattna broke into his reverie, "Papa, please come with me," she said, and took him to Anita's studio, while Anita was still asleep. In the medley of her mother's incomplete and vague paintings, she pointed out to him some distinct spots of brown which he knew were spots of coagulated blood. He knew what it was—Anita had not hurt herself—she had almost killed herself, and he was looking at the result of her alcoholism, a liver failure.

"Why did you not tell me before?" But Rattna did not answer. He sat there on the floor with his head between his knees, his heart sank, and tears poured from his eyes, and his world was dark.

"I brought this upon her," he said, "she depended on me. She is a simple woman with simple desires and simple aspirations. She joined me in my ambitious pursuits, for she loved me—she never wanted all this. She would have been happy just being a housewife, bringing up her child, painting beautiful sceneries, enjoying nature, shopping and perhaps gossiping with other simple women. The pressure of managing a hospital was too much for her, and she succumbed badly. I should have taken better care. I knew she was drinking heavily, but I did not bother to drag myself away from my work to spend time with her; to wean her away from alcohol, or arrange treatment for her, or at least let her live her life as she would have liked; instead I dragged her into living her life at my pace, and now I've nearly lost her. Her only fault is that she loves me, has always loved me, and just did what she thought would make me happy." And father and daughter both wept.

As the gravity of the situation dawned on him, he realized they had almost sunk beyond salvation. Taking Anita anywhere for treatment would mean almost the end of his own career; he was too well known in the community. Once word of her illness got out, the press would slaughter him with words; those he had paid to buy good press, would give him immensely bad press for free. Her parents were too old to help, or to bear the burden of her illness psychologically—they would die before their time, heartbroken.

All doctors were friends, and all doctors were foes, as in any other profession. One competitor going down uplifted their spirits as though his going down would mean them going up. But envy and greed are common to all men, and Amit wracked his brains to find a solution, to think of one person who could help him.

He requested the Germans to help him get his wife treated in Germany, keeping things under wraps, but they refused. He could not tell Ranee and Miss Mohan, for he needed to be in the health ministry's good books; options to get treatment in the US or Europe could not be considered, both for the high cost and the fact that he could not leave work to take her anywhere, and Rattna was in final year of college. She needed to work very hard. He felt like a total failure. He had done nothing for his wife, and she could be actually dying now. He did not know how bad her prognosis was till he could get the required tests done, but he didn't know where to go for those. Anyway, he decided to do the medical examination quickly, for he knew the value of time in such cases, and contacted an old friend from medical school, whom he convinced into secrecy, and spoke to Anita.

"I am sorry I have neglected you, but I can see your condition is not good at all. Please get ready and we shall go to my friend Raman's clinic. We need to do a thorough examination of your condition, to see how bad your liver is, and to begin therapy and de-addiction at once."

But Anita resisted, "There is nothing wrong with me," she said.

"Come on darling, I am a doctor, and I have seen the bloodstains you have unknowingly left in your studio; I can assess the situation clearly."

"Oh those!" said Anita, "I had bleeding gums, but now they are okay. I am absolutely fine, don't worry."

But Amit persevered and took her to Dr Raman's tiny clinic, and conducted her ultrasonography and also did an endoscopy, besides the numerous blood tests, confirming his worst fears. Close to seventy-five percent of her liver had been damaged, and he put his head on the table and wept like a baby. He sobbed till his whole body was contorted with grief. "I have hurt her the most whom I love the most. We have to save her, I cannot live without her; help me Raman." He cried and begged his friend to do something. After he was calmed, they both sat and discussed what action they could take, for Anita to be given the relevant treatment, and also for no one to find out. They decided to admit her in Raman's clinic itself. The staff was to be told that she was Raman's cousin whom he had brought from a small town to treat, for they did not have facilities in her home town. The chief mode of treatment was to wean her from the liquor, and to treat her liver with vitamins and steroids and other restructuring medications, the best possible, and give her ample relaxants and sedatives to help her fight the habit of drinking. She would be given lots of fluids to detoxify her blood and help her kidneys, and later she would be put on medicines which would help her feel repelled towards liquor. The bigger task was to convince Anita to take all this for she wanted to go home; she could not live without Rattna. She had to be sedated often, for when her pleadings did not work, she began to act hysterically, and tried to flee from the clinic; she wanted to be home, she wanted her drinks, and now she was getting terribly depressed too. Amit hated to be harsh with her, but her life was at stake, and she had to be treated.

In a few days, Anita seemed to have accepted her condition, and calmed down. She was accepting her medicines, and though restless, she was not demanding to be taken home. But even after a fortnight, her reports showed no improvement, her liver function test showed that her condition was actually slightly worse. Both Raman and Amit were worried, and discussed her case at length, but found that the medicines she was getting were the best, they could not improve on them. Amit requested Raman's wife, Sadhna, to come occasionally and be with Anita, so she would not feel too lonely and friendless, but strangely, Anita would be restless in her company. It seemed as if she was glad to be left alone, which made Sadhna wonder. She was the first one to guess that Anita had a regular supply of liquor and was drinking even at the clinic. They discovered that she had bribed the staff to get her the booze, and later dispense with the empty bottles, without anyone guessing; for, unlike other places, the smell of alcohol in a clinic does not surprise anyone. Now the situation for Amit became desperate, and as he sat with Raman and Sadhna, he could not think of anyone at all whom he could turn to—after all he could not strap his wife to a bed and have her guarded like a common drunkard.

Beas

SUDDENLY SADHNA sat up. She was recalling some distant memories, with her fingers rubbing her forehead, compiling them, and after a while she spoke, "What I am saying is really hearsay, but everything is worth investigating for us now. It comes to my mind that a distant cousin of mine had a problem with an alcoholic husband, and he was really bad. Recently, I met someone who is in touch with them, and asked about him, expecting the worst news, but I was told that he is fully cured and is now spending his life in helping others fight the problem. It seemed this family follows a sect of spiritual leaders, who are working round the globe, but their centre is near Amritsar, at a place called Beas, where their chief spiritual leader lives. He is said to be very powerful, and many people follow him. His work is as much social as it is spiritual, and he has been known to cure an amazingly large number of problems—social, spiritual and medical, and innumerable people have gained relief. Let me find out about this outfit and then I'll get you all details. Maybe we'll find succour at Beas."

With this tiny glimpse of a hope, they dispersed, and met again the next day. Sadhna did her research well, and was fully convinced that they would get help at Beas. "Babaji has a multi-acre Ashram there—actually he has one in almost every city in the country, and a hundred more abroad, and they are run totally by volunteers. Old people, sick people, lost and orphaned children, people with psychosomatic problems, people hunting for inner peace and spiritual guidance, all throng there, and get help. There are education centres, and medical care centres within the Ashram, manned by devoted and efficient staff. The therapy basically consists of taking part in the daily satsang, hearing Babaji's speeches or *Pravachan* as they are called, and simple and disciplined living, with a totally vegetarian diet. Since some years now, sensing the need, he has started a rehabilitation centre to cure people of drug and alcohol addiction. I found out that the Babaji right now happens to be in Beas, and have fixed a meeting with him for tomorrow evening. So if we take the morning flight to Amritsar, we can take a taxi and drive down to Beas by noon. If you can leave at short notice, that is." Amit jumped at the suggestion. The hospital and everything else was less important now—Anita's condition was his primary concern.

"Please kindly make the reservations at once, and book tickets for Rattna and one trusted nurse to go with us, for I cannot leave Rattna alone at home; Ranee also is away, and the nurse will stay with Anita, if we have to leave her there. So this is final; we all leave tomorrow, and let's hope for the best." In a corner of his mind, he could sense a small discomfort, for Ranee was returning from London the next day, and, for the first time, he felt like avoiding her, her scrutinising eyes, even her enthusiasm.

The appointment with Babaji was late evening, after the evening satsang, prayers, and his *pravachan*; after which he met all his followers, and last of all the ones who wanted a private discussion. It was a very tiring day for Anita, but the excitement of the journey and a new experience kept her in good spirits. Amit met Babaji alone, and shared Anita's problem with him, then Anita and the others came in for his blessings. When Anita tearfully bent to touch his feet, everyone heard her unspoken prayer, "Please help me Babaji. I want to live, I want to be happy, please cure me of my alcoholism, I am helpless, please help me...."

Babaji patted her head and said, " Pray to God, join in the service of the lesser endowed, spend your time with people who take His name, and sing his praises in the satsang, and the Almighty Father will grant you good health and happiness. We only have faith in His name, and His name is what we shall share with you to take you out of your suffering."

He told Amit, "You will have to leave Anita in the care of this Ashram for some months at least; there are many like her here. She will have no access to liquor from anywhere, and with a healthy diet, in the serene and peaceful surroundings, with friendly and kind people around her, she will surely recover. You will have to believe in us, and not communicate with her for some time, till she gets acclimatised to the discipline here. Later, you can talk to her often and even come to meet her, but only when I feel she is fit."

Amit folded his hands, bowed his head, and said, "I shall be always grateful to you. Please tell me how much money I should pay for the treatment, and also I shall leave a nurse with her to take care of her."

Babaji shut his eyes, then after a moment, he said, "There is no payment to be made for anything here; the coffers are constantly filled up by God himself through millions of unseen hands. We have plenty of dedicated volunteers who help the weak round the clock, better than their own family, with love and understanding. Thousands of followers of our sect have devoted their lives to serve in the Ashram for no remuneration. Service alone gives them satisfaction. Anita will be well cared for, and never left alone, be assured. Still, take your time and decide if you can leave her here, otherwise I shall simply bless you and you can go back home."

"I have no other hope now, Babaji, please take her in the Ashram, and help her get over her problem. I have only my gratitude to offer you, and though it will wring my heart, I will leave her in your care, and pray for her." This was all Amit could say. Babaji's presence made you feel so secure, you wanted to trust him as you would trust God himself. After a heart wrenching sleepless night, leaving Anita alone in this foreign place, they all left, trudging towards the cab.

As Anita awoke from the heavily sedated sleep, slightly groggy, she found herself all alone; she went to the door looking for Amit and Rattna, but the *sewadar* (volunteer), told her they had all left, and offered to get her some tea. Nobody disturbed her in the day except to get her meals, but when they brought her evening tea, they told her to take a bath and be dressed in time for the evening satsang. Everyone had to join in it unless one was totally bedridden. She was weak and low on stamina, but managed to go, though she could not sit through the whole ritual. She was ravaged by a craving for a drink. She walked back to her room, tormented by the pangs, each cell of her body crying out for some booze, her temples throbbing, hands trembling and the muscles of her legs paining and twitching at the same time. Reality dawned on her that she was almost imprisoned. But she had lots of money, and she checked. Her debit and credit cards were in her bag. She decided to wait for the people in the Ashram to settle down for they had an early dinner, and then she would try to organise something—to arrange for someone to get her some liquor.

When everyone seemed to have retired, she went out and requested the guards to go out and get her a bottle of brandy, saying that she needed it as medicine, but they refused. "No liquor of any type is allowed in the Ashram," they told her. She offered them huge tips, but they did not budge. Then she tried to go out herself, for the gates were all open. In fact, they always remained open, but some ladies came and gently escorted her back to her room. She begged, she wept, "Can't you see my condition? My whole body is rocked with pain. I have to get the brandy, try to understand. After some days, when your doctor has treated me, maybe I will be able to abstain, but now I need it. Take as much money as you like, but please get me some brandy. Your Babaji will never come to know, don't fear, and tomorrow I will work out something, and I won't bother you, but please for today, help me." Then a doctor came and gave her a sedative, while a lady sat in her room reciting some prayers, and rubbing her feet and legs to calm her down. But nothing helped. The sedative was too mild, and the lady's voice terribly irritating, Anita simply sobbed through the night, with not a wink of sleep.

The next day she again tried to leave the Ashram, planning to smuggle in some brandy, but despite the gates being open, and nobody apparently guarding them, some *sewadar* or other would appear and escort her back. By evening, she became hysterical. The phobia of the approaching night, and her torture of withdrawal symptoms, the awful craving for a drink, all became unbearable, and unlike herself, she lashed out at the *sewadars*. "This is an Ashram, not a prison. Here we are free to come and go, but you are treating me like a prisoner. My movements are fettered and I have no privacy. I came here of my own will, and I can leave of my own will—get out of my way."

The lady *sewadar* requested her to at least wish Babaji before she left, and gently steered her towards his room, where he sat with many new guests. Anita sat on the ground before him and he put his hand on her head in blessing, while he said, "I can understand the mental and physical torture you are going through, but you have to be strong. You have been slowly and slowly slipping into this deep pit for so many years, and now you have to climb back, which is very difficult; you have become physically so feeble and mentally so weak, that only your hidden spiritual strength will help you to climb back, and we all at the Ashram will help you. And you will win the fight, and be healthy and happy again. Come and join the sewadars here. You can help in the hospital giving medicines to patients, or in the tailoring hall, sewing on buttons and hooks, or in the community kitchen, in preparing the langar, whatever you feel strong enough to do. There are only two doses of medicine for you, *Simran*, which is the chanting of God's name, and *sewa* or community service. They are enough to treat all problems. Have faith, have courage and the strength will come."

"I will work in the langar; maybe I can shell some peas or chop some vegetables sitting on a chair," Anita said, quite reassured by what Babaji said.

All revolt left her then, and she decided to fight her problem, and after weeks of sleepless nights, nervous mornings, and sobbing afternoons, she began to feel some strength creeping back, some peace returning to her soul. Even the monotonous chopping of piles of spinach, aubergines and tomatoes was somehow very therapeutic; it had a calming influence on her, as her twitching hands got steadier and steadier. Chanting helped her sink her woes, and the polite care of the satsangis gave her confidence. She began to fall in love with these serene surroundings—rows of bougainvillas in different colours, the gentle breeze, noiseless atmosphere as nobody even wore shoes that made a sound—all helped in her therapy. She was sure she would soon be fully recovered, though some days she did crave for a drink, but she was creating structures that would help her fight that craving. There was a lot of hope now. She still did not get much sleep, but whenever she looked out of her room, she saw people occupied in some service or other, constantly cleaning, scrubbing and washing the corridors and verandas, the prayer halls and large cooking vessels, or simply sitting alone and meditating, and soon she began to do the same, as she regained more strength, and felt more peaceful.

But it was tough, very tough. She spent the scorching summer nights sobbing into her pillow. In the monsoon, the sound of raindrops on the roof created a clatter in her throbbing brain; and the long winter nights and dull winter days left her hopelessly depressed; but she persevered with Babaji's therapy and the regimen of the Ashram, and by the time spring came, she began to ask Amit to get her paints and easels. She now wished to paint—she wished to paint the colours of a new horizon. She wished to share her story through the colours of her palette, to tell of a rebirth almost happening, and wanted to grow again. She was missing home, and missing Rattna, but knew she ought to remain here still. As for Rattna, Anita was reassured since she knew that Rattna had found her mentor in Miss Mohan, and they both communicated often, and that Miss Mohan was guiding her well at this crucial stage of her life, both to get into the career she wanted and to be a strong and righteous lady. 'God gives us millions of small graces, before we even know that we need them,' Anita thought.

Greater heights

RANEE RETURNED from London, full of euphoria and excitement. She had got a much better response than she had believed she could, and wanted to share it all with Amit. Also the implementation of several new measures to meet the new traffic of patients, but was surprised that he had chosen to take a holiday at this juncture. She spoke to him on the phone and he told her to begin making the new plans with Dr Meena Madhok till he returned, for a large number of patients were expected to come for IVF treatment and deliveries. There was a great demand for surrogate pregnancies from UK because the law there did not allow them to be conducted. Indian laws were liberal on this issue. If a woman could not carry her baby due to some malfunction in her uterus or some other reason, she could have her ovum fertilized by her husband's sperm, and literally 'hire' another woman's womb to carry her baby by having the embryo implanted in her uterus, till a successful delivery was conducted and then, the newborn was handed over to it's natural parents. These surrogates would invariably be in need of money, and they would be amply rewarded monetarily, with the doctors getting a hefty cut too. But women from UK, who craved the elusive motherhood, gladly paid for a surrogate, and rewarded the doctors well, and were themselves well rewarded with a child. A satisfying situation for all.

Then there were the women who had healthy wombs but malfunctioning ovaries; there was a remedy for them too for India had plenty of donors for ova too. Nature has devised a perfect system for reproduction in human beings. Coinciding with the time when the uterus is in the best condition to accept and nurture a new embryo, the woman's ovaries which contain the ova, alternating their function every month, are ready with one matured ovum, which bursts out of its follicle and starts a journey towards the fallopian tube, where mostly it gets fertilized by a sperm, and then it gets attached to the lining of the uterus, to grow to be a baby, a human being. When a woman has no ova in her ovaries, or there is some other medical condition, meriting the use of a donor's ova, a donor is sought out, very carefully. India being a land of many races, a donor is chosen well so that the resulting child does not look totally unlike the recipient parents, and for an agreeable compensation, unless out of love or friendship, which is very rare, used for ovum donation. She is pumped with hormones, so that she has a healthy ovum ready, and to make sure that a pregnancy does result, she is given enough hormones to have several ova maturing in a single period. Mostly there are seven to eight follicles giving forth, and sometimes even up to twelve have been 'cropped' in a single month of hormone treatment. The IVF surgeon takes out these ova surgically, at the optimum time, uses two or more of them to fertilize them with the sperm that have been already collected. He implants them in the patient's uterus, hoping that at least one of these embryos', fertilized in the laboratory, attaches itself to the fertile lining of the recipient mother's uterus leading to a successful pregnancy. Often, though, two or more pregnancies result, then the ones growing most healthy are retained.

Ranee connived with Meena to make some extra money among themselves. Between the two of them, they created a secret 'ovum bank'. If they paid, say, fifty thousand rupees to the donor for one ovarian cycle, to retrieve her ova once, and they got more than the required number of ova, they would file the data regarding the woman and freeze the extra ova. The next time a patient needed a matching donor, they would use the preserved ova, while not paying for it, but still charging the receiving person a huge amount. With greater precision in their technique, they were able to provide up to three patients from a single donor, while they earned three times over or more, depending upon the desperation and paying capacity of the patients. They learned to do the same with sperm donors. While paying for a single sperm donation, they used the retrieved sperm for several pregnancies, after matching the profiles of the receiving parents.

Again, in these matters, most recipients were very secretive and requested the doctors to be secretive too, and pretended that either they had a natural pregnancy, or that the sperm and ovum which gave forth the IVF pregnancy were those of the couple involved. This suited Meena and Ranee perfectly. It became even better when crowds of women from the Middle Eastern countries began to throng their clinic. The culture of these countries sets great importance for a woman to have children. Women are even afraid of losing their marital status, or their husbands marrying again, if they cannot have a child. And they are ready to pay anything to someone who will help them get pregnant. The problem here would be more about finding donors for ova and sperm, for it would be difficult to find women and men to match the appearance, complexion, build and other traits of these couples, which is important if the couple does not wish to make it public that a donor has been used to achieve the pregnancy. Since these are affluent countries, and women do not venture out alone, so finding women donors was indeed a problem. But Ranee and Meena worked around it by freezing and later using the extra ova retracted from women who came for their own IVF treatments. As also the sperm of genuine patients. Amit was anyway distraught, his house was in shambles, and the Gynae department was already being run by Meena Madhok, who now, was aided by Ranee, who was in charge of marketing.

Amit was getting plenty of knee transplant and other joint replacement patients from abroad, and word of mouth publicity, and the kickbacks offered by Ranee to co-operating doctors from these countries was paying well. Money was rolling in, and everybody was getting richer. A lot richer than they had ever imagined they could be. Which was a good thing but too much unprecedented wealth often gives rise to complacence, euphoria, and over confidence.

Early one morning, Rattna walked to her father's room to wish him before leaving for college, and seeing that he was in the shower, was about to quietly leave, when Ranee breezed in from the dressing room and swished into the bathroom, joining him in the shower, leaving Rattna stunned and shocked. Like a zombie, she trudged back to her room, and sat like a statue for hours; nobody came looking for her as they all thought she had left for college. At noon, the lady came in to clean the room and still found her sitting like a stone. Thinking she was missing her mother, she hugged her, trying to give her solace, but Rattna said, "Please leave me alone, I have to study."

By evening, she had assessed the situation and come to terms with it, so at dinner she told Amit, "May I please shift to the room upstairs? I have to study a lot while preparing for my college and the IAS exams. Since no one comes up there I can keep whatever hours I like, and work undisturbed. Also, please don't mind if I cannot sometimes come down for dinner; my studies are my priority now." Next morning, she shifted her books and her clothes to the single room on the terrace, and limited her communication with everyone. She frequently spoke to Miss Mohan, who was her guide for her career and her life in general, and Miss Mohan in turn loved her for her sincerity, hard work and sensitivity, and took her under her wing with enthusiasm and vigour. She knew this girl would rise to great heights, for she had inner strength and courage, even in adversity.

Teheran, Iran

ABDUL MUBARAK was very happy to be back in Teheran. After several years, his country, Kuwait, and Iran had decided to exchange Ambassadors and augment the consulates in both countries, to further improve trade, and cultural and educational exchange between them. He had lived in Teheran as a child, when his father had been an Ambassadorial attaché, but when the war with Iraq started, they had to leave, for relations among the two countries had soured. He had had a very happy childhood in Teheran, lots of friends among the kids of his father's colleagues, and also the foreign officers from other countries, for most of these 'consular' children, as they were called, went to the same school, the Daneshmand High School,the best in Iran. They were all very friendly, and as much as he enjoyed his friends, he loved the cool weather too. He never forgot Rasool Iqbal, his best friend, whose family had a huge villa in Teheran, and were said to be a very old, prosperous and highly learned family. Iqbal and Mubarak had been inseparable in school, and when he had joined the foreign office in Kuwait after his education, he had always dreamt of relations between Kuwait and Iran improving, and he being lucky enough to be posted there. Well, wishes did become horses, and Mubarak was indeed back in Teheran, after a gap of nearly thirty years.

After settling down, the first thing he did was to find Iqbal, which was not difficult, and both quickly caught up again, for Iqbal had missed him just as much. They spent hours reliving the childhood years, and talking about what else happened in between. They searched the market for the fruits and nuts they used to munch in school, and soon became inseparable again. Their lives had followed the predictable pattern. Iqbal had joined his family business and Mubarak had joined the foreign office, like his father. Both had married and had children of about the same age. Mubarak felt sure when his family joined him in Teheran, both families would bond well together; their wives had already become facebook friends.

Some time later, Iqbal invited Mubarak to join him on a trip to Isfahan where his sister Zubeida was celebrating her children's second birthday. She had been blessed with twins, a boy and a girl, after thirteen years of marriage, and Iqbal's whole family would make the trip to celebrate with her. Mubarak went along, but asked Iqbal if the two of them could go a couple of days earlier than the others, for he had never visited Isfahan, and wanted to go sightseeing. When they reached, Zubeida told them to freshen up first and then they would all have tea together. Then she brought her kids to meet them. And Mubarak felt as though he was struck by a rock on his head. Zubeida's daughter was the spit image of his own sister, Haseena, who lived in Kuwait. He looked on, dazed, as Iqbal hugged the two kids one by one, then hugged them both together, as Mubarak's head spun, wondering how it was possible. When they came to say *salaam* to him, he too hugged them, and looking behind the girl's neck, saw that she had the identical birthmark that all women born in his family had. He was stunned. The first possibility that came to his mind was that perhaps Zubeida's husband had some ancestry in common with his family, but upon enquiring that was ruled out at once. Then he wondered if Zubeida may have had an affair with someone in his family, but no possible connection occurred to him. Besides, when he brought the conversation to travelling, he was told that Zubeida had never left the country. But the birthmark was the clincher, the resemblance could not be just by chance.

Perplexed, he began his own subtle enquiries. His gut feeling was that there had to be a plausible explanation. Being in the government service gave you access to a lot of information, whether in your own department, or through friends in other departments or other ministries. Some people were appointed by him to conduct discreet enquiry about the different family trees, the activity of the two families, their movements, travels, literally all they could do to get a thorough detection and investigation. He could not believe two human beings could be so identical without there being some connection at least. And he would not rest till he found the truth. He was determined.

Suddenly, a mail came in demanding urgent attention. One operative's finding had thrown up some interesting details. The travel details of the two families, Zubeida's and Haseena's, showed similar activity. Both couples had travelled to a major city in India, lived in the same hotels, paid huge bills to the same hospital and to a certain guest house. Both had travelled there three times, twice in one month, with the third trip lasting three months. But the trips of the two families had been a year apart, and had nothing else in common. Mubarak knew he would find his answer somewhere in this information, but nothing fitted with any hypothesis he could imagine, until he saw what the hospital was; it was a destination for mainly orthopaedic transplants, organ transplants, and IVF treatments.

IVF treatments! That would explain why Zubeida denied having travelled out of the country. If she had had her babies by the IVF method, she may be wishing to keep it a secret, especially if they had used a donor; and his mind raced at top speed. Maybe there was a donor, and that donor was connected to his own family. That was it, for sure. They had probably got a sperm or ovum by donation and were obviously concealing it. That was why he did not know that his sister had also gone to India. When the possible and most probable reality stared him in the face, he was stunned. The most impossible possibilities reared their head in his mind like futuristic monsters.

Pondering all night, he decided he should be sure of his suspicions and have some concrete proof before he shared things with anyone. So he travelled to Kuwait and arranged for a detective to work as a waiter at a restaurant where he invited his sister's family to dinner. The detective was instructed to whisk away his sister's plate pretending to see an imaginary sliver of hair on it. He would use her used spoon to pick up some saliva for DNA testing. Similarly, he contrived a trick to collect some material from Iqbal's sister's daughter. Here luck simply favoured him; his operative was working at Zubeida's house as a domestic help trying desperately to get the little girl to spit on something, or waiting if she would get hurt while playing so he could get a swab of her blood. The opportunity came quite soon when she fell from the swing and scraped her knee. The operative cleaned the wound and rushed with the swab to Mubarak, who immediately sent it to his department to be sent secretly for a DNA matching test. He spent sleepless nights waiting for the report, which gave the two a perfect match. They were mother and daughter undoubtedly, said the report.

He didn't have to be Einstein to make four out of two and two. He composed himself and began a plan of action. He shared his findings with high officials in his department. Ministers were contacted and convinced. Hotlines between ministries of the three countries really hotted up, and though the matter was kept top secret, 'Aman Nursing Home' was immediately put under severe security surveillance. CBI was brought in and their most senior officers and cyber experts were appointed to investigate the case. All sorts of electronic security, tapping of phones, scanning of emails, even scanning of posted and couriered letters and documents was carried out. A no holds barred approach followed. Pinhead sized cameras, recording devices, all were used. Doctors went in pretending to be staff of the outsourced housekeeping services; investigation officers went in pretending to be patients; and policemen were attending to customers at the cafeteria and the chemist shops. People with sharp eyes and ears and immense observation skills made up the 'human' surveillance team, and helped in coming to various conclusions about what went on in the hospital. A hospital, like a railway train, is one place where people tend to open up to total strangers about their lives. Everything was observed and noted.

It did not take too long to find and provide sufficient reasons for the Foreign Ministry, Ministry of Home Affairs, and Health Ministry to get together and register a special case with the CBI. Needless to say, the CBI decided to take action at once.

The people at Aman Nursing Home—Amit, Meena and all the other surgeons and staff were in for the biggest shock of their lives, when the CBI officials appeared and flashed their cards, and asked them all to literally put their hands up, and "Please co-operate in the investigations."

Last Chapter

DR SINHA was appointed the chief surveyor and inspector by the Health Ministry and Central Bureau of Investigation together, to get to the root of whatever illegal practices were taking place at Aman Nursing Home. She occupied a room on the ground floor along with her team of investigating officers, backed by a large group of IT technicians collecting data, sifting it, filtering it and passing it on to her team, for investigation. She allowed the hospital to continue to work as it did, except she appointed some twenty special guards throughout the whole building, to make sure not even a slip of paper left the premises, or was destroyed in any way. These guards were chosen for their integrity and dedication, and though in plain clothes, were armed to the hilt. Meanwhile, the Germans upstairs quietly escaped and Amit's contacts in Germany broke off all communication channels with him. He tried emails but they would not go across, his calls were blocked out; for him they had suddenly disappeared. Ranee never returned to the hospital. She took a cab to the airport lest her car be followed, and with some clothes and a toothbrush, her passport and bank cards, flew out of the country. Later, she would assess the situation, which was going to be very bad, for she knew how thorough Dr Sinha's team was; but she did have loads of money stashed away abroad.

Hearing about this Miss Mohan at once came to be with the family, and assured Dr Sinha that she could count on her co-operation and also her daughter's, whenever needed. She would not leave till the case was solved. This gesture was greatly appreciated by Dr Sinha as Miss Mohan had been a very senior colleague. Miss Mohan also wished to be with Rattna whom she had mentored and taken under her wing. This was going to be Rattna's most serious ordeal and Miss Mohan had to be with her giving her love and moral support.

Diligently, Dr Sinha had her sleuths go through every drawer and cupboard, every crevice where something could be hidden, tapped the floor and roof for hollow spaces, shook every man and woman of the staff with their questioning, and got out important information. Within a week, some clarity began to form about this rare case. She did not miss anything—from the false bills to the blank X-rays, the ICU medicine records to the enormous turnover of the Gynaecology department. She was shocked by what she was seeing. It was both phenomenal and scandalising. The number of innocent people who had been cheated depressed her, and she was surprised that the man who left out no malpractice had left the organ trade alone. It was unbelievable and she questioned Amit non-stop, but he did not commit to any offence. He was a tough nut.

She persevered with both, questioning and finding old and incriminating documents, and wondered why he would have retained those after so many years. She did not then know that Amit was a stickler for his accounts and wanted to be very sure he got his proper due from the Germans. Therefore, he maintained old records, in case at some point of time they suppressed his payments. Old case files showed gaping holes between cost and procedure; only a doctor of Dr Sinha's calibre could see through it. Commercial records were almost like confessions; no trouble had been taken to camouflage their misdeeds, except to conceal them and stow them away. One did not need Dr Sinha's expertise to see it. She realized Amit must have enjoyed heavy political clout and greased many Income Tax or more important Health Ministry inspectors, for no questions ever seemed to have been asked.

The super secretive Germans too, though they were very careful and concealed their faces within the hospital, did leave some of their pictures on some random closed circuit cameras, in moments of carelessness. Nobody remembered the cctv camera Amit had installed in the building opposite his own, which would have been effective in case of a robbery or an attack on the hospital, as it would have caught the escaping criminals' faces. In the event of anything like that never happening, that camera was duly forgotten and never looked into. In the footage of this particular camera, Dr Sinha found the faces of several Germans. These were sent to the Emigration authorities at the airport and all the men were soon identified, and copies of their passports passed on to her. It turned out that they were not even 'Germans'. Amit had been taken for such a ride; they belonged to different East European countries and some South African countries. Their data and their email accounts showed up, and when the telecom and internet service providers were prevailed upon by the Health Minister himself, the internet and other electronic transactions of all these men through the years gave them information that filled up servers. The analysis of this vital information left everybody aghast.

These people had, over the years, built up a network of small time physicians, and nursing homes in big and small towns, to conduct trials of several drugs undergoing research in the labs in some highly developed countries, and for some leading pharmaceutical companies, on unsuspecting patients without their knowledge or approval.

Drugs for tuberculosis, gonorrhoea and syphilis, respiratory and heart diseases, nephrological syndromes, types of influenza, infertility and birth-control, AIDS , meningitis; the list was very long. Tons of these drugs must have been circulated around the country's unsuspecting poor and rich alike, and the findings reported to the men in Amit's hospital. They located labs in some remote hill towns, where embryos were being created in test-tubes, to crop them for stem cells, which were sent abroad for research through a series of carriers and transit facilitators. It was appalling. It came to light that in one village, a young boy, retarded at birth due to cerebral palsy, had turned into a monster after the technician at the lab injected him with stem cells, conducting an experiment of his own, having heard of such trials being done elsewhere around the world. It was the biggest scandal in free India, the biggest in any country maybe, made possible because of one man's greed, one man's carelessness. It was an assault on the country's freedom, an act against the state. For want of better vocabulary, Dr Sinha called it, "Medical Espionage and Biological Warfare." No one knew how many thousands of sick people had been denied the relevant treatment, while experimental drugs were tried on them, whereas overdose of drugs would have rendered others permanently immune to medication. It went beyond imagination that a whole generation of the poor and lower middle class population of the country had been used like guinea pigs by these unscrupulous men.

Several international investigation agencies, police departments of many countries, Interpol, all came together to frame charges against Amit Biswas, Anita Biswas and Meena Madhok. They were arrested at midnight, and charged with FEMA, Income Tax violation, for Medical Misdeeds and Malpractices, compromising National Security, and unethical and illegal trials of drugs.

When the news broke in the media, Babaji in Beas was terribly shaken. He could not forgive himself for not recognising Amit and Anita for the beasts they were. He came to the city to meet them, and requested them to confess their crimes and beg forgiveness from the citizens of India, but before that he had to take the permission of Dr Sinha. Miss Mohan was there too and when they met, recognition dawned on them both, and Miss Mohan folded her hands and bowed to him for a blessing. He said, "I had blessed you, and you have risen very high with your hard work, honesty and integrity. But I had told you to never take what was not yours, and you did not listen, now see how much hurt and sorrow it has caused you. When you go against God's wishes, it only brings sorrow." And then she understood. It had not been in her fate to be a mother; Babaji's warning proved to be a prophecy.

The foreign company seemed to never have existed. There was a factory at the premises mentioned in the papers found with Amit, but it was involved in regular legal work; they could find nothing questionable about it. None of the directors or managers mentioned were to be traced anywhere; Amit had been taken for a ride. Dr Sinha's hunch was that it was an international drug mafia, manufacturing drugs and conducting research for some terrorist states in some under developed countries which had become havens for illegal activity. Nobody would have the audacity and acumen to undertake such a project and go undiscovered in a powerful and well governed country like Germany. Stupid Amit did not even know whom he was really working for; but the Indian government with the help of international agencies would find out soon.

Ranee had not been chargesheeted for they found no incriminating evidence against her, though inducing people and knowledge of illegal activity going on and not reporting it, is a crime in itself. They were taking time to decide how to indict her. Though for all practical purposes she had gone underground, she believed some of the powerful people she knew would help her to go untraced. But she also knew her mother well. And when her phone rang, she knew it was Mamma.

"Ranee, my child," said Miss Mohan, "I want you back fast, and in good health." Before she replied, all the options ran through her mind; she could escape to another country, have a change of identity, even marry one of the powerful sheikhs in the Middle East and they would ensure she would never be seen by anyone she did not want to; or she could simply commit suicide. But Mamma's voice inside her said that she would never be a coward. "Ok Mamma, I love you," she replied, "I'll be back soon."

Where else could she ever hope to be secure, except with her Mamma!